# DEADLY BARGAIN

"I usually hunt animals," Vin Hacker said. "To kill a man is gonna cost you extra."

"I'll pay extra, don't worry," Mayor Masters said. "That's one and two, the wolf and Holt."

"And Adams?"

"He's number three. I don't need word getting out about what's going on in this town. To keep Holt from talking—or Adams—I'll pay whatever it will take."

"What do you want done about Adams?"

"Whatever it takes to keep him quiet," Masters said. "When it's done, come and see me and we'll settle up. Okay?"

Hacker hesitated, then said, "Sure, but I need some pocket money."

"I thought you might," Masters said. He took an envelope out of his desk and tossed it across to Hacker's side. The wolfer picked it up and tucked it away inside his skins somewhere without counting it.

"Can you handle Adams?" Masters asked.

"I'll handle him."

# DON'T MISS THESE
## ALL-ACTION WESTERN SERIES
## FROM THE BERKLEY PUBLISHING GROUP

*THE GUNSMITH by J. R. Roberts*

Clint Adams was a legend among lawmen, outlaws, and ladies. They called him . . . the Gunsmith.

*LONGARM by Tabor Evans*

The popular long-running series about U.S. Deputy Marshal Long—his life, his loves, his fight for justice.

*LONE STAR by Wesley Ellis*

The blazing adventures of Jessica Starbuck and the martial arts master, Ki. Over eight million copies in print.

*SLOCUM by Jake Logan*

Today's longest-running action Western. John Slocum rides a deadly trail of hot blood and cold steel.

# THE GUNSMITH

## 150

### NIGHT OF THE WOLF

## J. R. ROBERTS

JOVE BOOKS, NEW YORK

NIGHT OF THE WOLF

A Jove Book / published by arrangement with
the author

PRINTING HISTORY
Jove edition / June 1994

ISBN: 0-515-11393-X

A JOVE BOOK®
Jove Books are published by The Berkley Publishing Group,
200 Madison Avenue, New York, New York 10016.
JOVE and the "J" design are trademarks belonging to Jove Publications, Inc.

PRINTED IN THE UNITED STATES OF AMERICA

10  9  8  7  6  5  4  3  2  1

# THE GUNSMITH

150

## NIGHT OF THE WOLF

# ONE

The first thing Clint saw were the traces of red on the snow. Instinctively, he knew that they were blood. They were washed out, not vivid, because the snow had started to swallow them up. It was blood, though. He had seen enough of it to know, and the horses—his team and Duke—could smell it.

"Easy," he said, speaking to the team.

They were spooked, and not easily soothed, which led him to believe that it was something other than the blood that was making them nervous. The only other thing he could figure was that they were smelling a wild animal—a bear or, even more likely, a wolf. In fact, he'd seen some wolf tracks further back, had stopped and stepped down from his rig to inspect them. They were easily the largest tracks he had ever seen left by a wolf.

The team never stopped. He wouldn't let them. He kept them moving until he saw something lying in the snow ahead of them.

1

A man.

Well, a body, anyway. Dead or alive he didn't know yet. He directed the team closer, but at one point they stopped and stubbornly refused to move.

There were still those traces of blood in the snow, leading up to the body. They were deeper red now, and even he could smell the blood. He didn't blame the team for not wanting to get closer.

He finally left them alone and dropped down from the rig. He walked around to the back first to make sure that Duke was okay. There was a lot of white showing in the big gelding's eyes, but Clint put his hand on the animal's massive neck and spoke to him.

"Take it easy, big boy," he said. "I'll just go and take a look."

Duke's reins were tied to the back of the wagon, and before moving away Clint untied them. If anything went wrong he wanted the gelding to be free to get away—or to help, whichever the case might be.

That done, he walked away from his rig toward the body in the snow. Judging from the amount of blood he had followed to here, and what was in the snow now, he doubted that the person would still be alive. Still, he had to check.

As he got closer, he saw the deep red in the snow around the body. He kept alert, looking around for any sign of movement. There were trees, but none thick enough to hide anyone—

or anything. He could see for miles, except for an occasional dip or rise in the ground. If a bear or a wolf approached, he'd be able to see it in time.

He reached the body and leaned down. The blood was thick around the dead man, and as Clint turned the body over he saw that the throat had been torn out. Not cut with a knife, but torn away, as if with razor-sharp teeth.

Not a bear, he decided, looking down at the dead man. Probably a wolf.

The man's eyes were wide open, and there were indications in the snow that he had walked and then dragged himself. There were also some wolf tracks. From the tracks Clint reconstructed what must have happened.

The man had probably been attacked by the wolf, wounded, and then escaped. He ran, with the wolf tracking him. Eventually the animal had caught up with him and finished him off.

Clint knew little about wolves, but he did know that they did not usually attack without some provocation. He wondered if the man had been hunting the wolf, and if the hunter had found himself to be the hunted.

The man's face—where it was visible from behind a heavy beard—was pale, as if drained of blood. The cheeks were sunken, and Clint couldn't be sure if they had been that way in life. Dead, the man looked old, maybe in his late fifties or early sixties. Clint felt sure that he was significantly younger than that in life, though. Death had a way of aging a person.

He checked the man's body for identification and found none. The man had a holster on, but it was empty. In one pocket Clint found shells for a rifle, but when he searched the area, he couldn't locate a rifle.

"Poor bastard," he said aloud.

He would've liked to have buried the man, but he did not for several reasons. One was that the ground was too cold and hard to dig a grave. Another reason was there was no telling if that wolf was still in the area. His animals were skittish, which meant they smelled the blood in the snow, and maybe the wolf too.

The third reason was that he was about a mile outside of a town called Molasses, Montana. He could notify the sheriff when he got to town, and then the lawman could send someone out to collect the body. Once the body was taken into town, a proper burial could be arranged.

Clint walked back to his rig where he patted both of the horses in his team and spoke soothingly to them. Suddenly he stopped and looked around. He had the eerie feeling that he was being watched, but by whom—or what?

"Time to get going," he said, to himself and to the horses.

He climbed back aboard his rig and started the team in the direction of town. They were difficult to handle until he steered them around the bloodied body. Duke followed behind, still untethered, but Clint knew that the black gelding would go where he went.

Right now he was heading for Molasses.

# TWO

He had gone only a half mile when he saw the second body.

It had occurred to him—albeit briefly—that the amount of blood he had seen might not have come from one person. The sighting of the second body seemed to confirm that. However, there was no blood in the snow here, nor was the scent of blood in the air; the team was as calm as they had been since leaving the other body behind.

There was a possibility, then, that this body—this person—might still be alive.

He was able to take the rig closer to this body before dropping to the ground to take a look. It was a man, and as he put his hand on one shoulder to turn him over, Clint heard a groan.

He gently turned the man onto his back. Like the first man this one was bearded, but he was alive. His eyelids fluttered as he looked up at Clint.

"Wha—" he said. "What's—where is it?"

"Where's what?"

The man's eyes flicked around, then settled back on Clint again.

"I'm cold."

"Are you hurt?"

"I . . . don't know."

"What happened?" Clint asked. "Was anyone with you?"

"I . . . I'm cold."

Clint decided that questioning the man could wait until later.

"All right," he said. "Let's get you into the back of my rig. I've got some blankets there."

The man closed his eyes and nodded, and it was several seconds before he opened them again. Longer—much longer—than a blink, but at least he was still conscious.

Clint put his hands beneath the man's arms and helped him to his feet. There were no visible wounds on the man, but he was obviously too weak to walk on his own. Clint half carried and half dragged him to the back of his rig, them boosted him inside.

He climbed in after him, found a couple of blankets, and wrapped the man in them.

"I'm sorry," he said to the man, "I have nothing warm to offer you to drink."

"That's . . . okay," the man said. "This is . . . much better."

"Wait," Clint said, suddenly remembering a half bottle of whiskey he had somewhere. He rooted around in the back of the rig before finding it.

"Here."

He held the bottle to the man's lips and lifted it. The man took some of the whiskey into his mouth and swallowed it. Clint knew that would at least burn, if not warm him inside.

"Can you tell me your name?" Clint asked.

The man's eyelids fluttered and then suddenly closed. After a moment, Clint lifted an eyelid to take a look and satisfied himself that the man had passed out.

"Okay," he said, "I'll find out your name later. Right now let's get into town."

He climbed over the front of the rig and settled back in the driver's seat.

"Come on," he said to his team, lifting the reins and snapping them, "let's get going. I'm starting to get the willies out here."

The team started forward, and Clint shook the reins to get them moving faster. He still felt like he was being watched. It was a feeling he'd had before, but never like this. There were times when he knew by instinct that someone—some person—was watching him, but this didn't feel like those times. This felt different, and he didn't like it.

He didn't like it one damn bit.

# THREE

The man in the back of the rig did not stir during the half mile ride to town. As Clint directed his team down the main street of the oddly named Molasses, Montana, he felt himself relax, but the team remained tense. He found that strange. All the team would smell—or *should* smell—in town was people and other horses. No wolf in his right mind would come into a town full of people. Why, then, was the team still skittish?

He pulled his rig to a halt in the middle of the street and hailed a man who was crossing.

"You got a doctor in town?"

"Sure do," the man said, pointing. "Doc Craddock. His office is over next to the general store."

"And what about the sheriff?"

"Got one of them too," the man said. "He's a couple of streets past the doc, same side."

"Thanks," Clint said.

He was surprised at the size of Molasses. Somehow a town by that name did not conjure up visions of a bustling, well-populated place.

He snapped the reins and walked the team over to the general store. Next to it he saw a door with a shingle on it that read: DOCTOR T. CRADDOCK.

He walked around to the back of the rig, wondering if the man inside was even still alive. He hadn't made a sound or moved since Clint had given him the whiskey.

He climbed into the back and established that the man was still breathing, and then left him there while he went into the doctor's office.

Doc Craddock was in his seventies if he was a day. The old sawbones looked up from a rolltop desk as Clint entered his office.

"Stranger in town," the doc said. It was a statement, not a question.

"That's right," Clint said, "and I've got some business for you—that is, if you're the doctor."

"I am," Craddock said. "Where are you hurtin'?"

"I'm not," Clint said. "My name's Clint Adams, Doc. I got a man out in my rig who is hurtin'. I found him lying in the snow about half a mile outside of town."

"Well then, bring him in," Craddock said. "I can't do him much good if you leave him out there, can I?"

"No, I guess not," Clint said. "I'll get him."

Clint went out, figuring he'd have to drag the man out of his rig alone without any help from the doc. He was surprised when the old man followed him outside.

"That your rig?" Craddock asked.

"That's right."

"What's your business?"

"Gunsmith."

The doc nodded and followed Clint around behind the rig.

Clint got in and sat the man up so the doc could see his face.

"Know him?"

"I know him," Craddock said. "His name's Ned Holt. Get him out of there."

Clint pulled Holt to the rear of the rig, then dropped down and pulled the man out after him. Holt's eyes flickered and his legs held under him some. Not enough to walk, but enough so that Clint didn't have to carry him.

"Get him inside," Craddock said.

Clint and Holt followed the doctor inside. They went through the office into a second room.

"Where's he hurt?" Craddock asked.

"I don't know."

"Put him on the examining table."

Clint got Holt to the table and laid him out on it.

"Get some of those clothes off of him."

"I've got to find the sheriff, Doc," Clint said.

"What for?"

"There's a second man out there, about a mile outside of town."

"Why didn't you bring him in?"

"He's dead already."

"Oh," Craddock said.

He walked to the table and looked down at the semiconscious man.

"All right," he said finally, "I can get him undressed. Go and talk to the sheriff."

"What's the sheriff's name?"

"Bennett," the doc said, "Horace Bennett."

"A good man?" Clint asked.

"He'll do," Craddock said. "Get out of here now and let me do my job."

"I'll stop back after I see the sheriff," Clint said. "I'm curious—"

"Do what you want after," Craddock said, "but leave me be with my patient now, hear?"

"I hear," Clint said and left.

Out front he debated whether or not to drive his rig over to the sheriff's office, then decided to leave it where it was. He did, however, mount Duke and ride the big gelding the two blocks to the sheriff's office.

# FOUR

Clint entered the sheriff's office and looked at the man seated behind the desk. Actually, there were two desks. One was against the wall opposite the door, and one was to Clint's left. The one on the left was empty. Sheriff Horace Bennett was seated at the one opposite the door. He was a big, red-faced man, probably in his late thirties, with a heavy black mustache and an equally heavy beard that did nothing to hide his double chin.

"Can I help you?" the lawman asked.

"Sheriff Bennett?"

"That's right."

Clint approached the man's desk.

"My name's Clint Adams," he said. "I just arrived in town and brought with me an injured man. I found him about half a mile south of town."

"Who we talkin' about?" Bennett asked.

"The doctor—Doc Craddock—he says the man's name is Ned Holt."

12

"Ned?" Bennett said. "Hurt? What happened to him?"

"Well, that's just it. I don't know. He's over at the doc's now getting looked at."

"Was he shot?"

"No," Clint said, "there's no wound."

"Knifed?"

"Like I said," Clint went on, shaking his head, "there's no wound that I could see."

"Well then, what happened to him?"

"I don't know, Sheriff," Clint said patiently. "The doctor is trying to find that out now."

"Hmm," Bennett said, frowning.

"Does he have family?" Clint asked.

"Ned? Oh yeah, he's got a wife and kids, and a sister . . . Rachel."

There was something dreamy about the sheriff's eyes when he said the sister's name. It made Clint think that maybe this Rachel was something special to the man—or maybe the sheriff wanted her to be.

"Maybe you should notify them, and they could go over to the doctor's and get him."

"They live in a house outside of town," Bennett said. "I'll have to send someone out to talk to them—or maybe go myself."

"As long as somebody tells them," Clint said. "And there's something else."

"What?"

"I found another man," Clint said, "about a mile out of town, same direction."

The sheriff narrowed his eyes as he stared at Clint with something akin to suspicion now. A stranger in town five minutes reporting that he's found two injured men. Well, maybe Clint could understand the man's attitude.

"He hurt too?"

"No," Clint said, "he's dead."

"Dead?" Bennett said, raising his eyebrows. "Know who he is?"

"I'm a stranger around here, Sheriff," Clint said. "I didn't know him."

"Oh, that's right," Bennett said. The man did not seem particularly sharp. Clint wondered about the doctor's remark that he was good enough for the job.

"Did he have any identification on him?" Bennett asked. "Anything that would tell you who he was?"

Clint debated for a moment whether he should admit he went through the man's pockets, but then decided to simply tell the truth.

"None that I could find."

"Did you look?"

"I went through his pockets."

"Did you take anything?"

"Sheriff," Clint said, trying to control his temper, "if I had taken anything, would I admit to you that I went through his pockets?"

"No," Bennett said, frowning, "I guess not. How was he killed? Was he shot?"

"He was killed by an animal."

"An animal?" Bennett said. The expression on his face changed. He now looked . . . apprehensive. "What kind of animal?"

"I don't know," Clint said. "I saw some wolf

tracks near the body, though. Have you been having trouble hereabouts with wolves?"

Bennett didn't answer the question. Instead he asked one of his own.

"Exactly how was he killed?"

"His throat was torn out," Clint said. "Obviously by some kind of animal. I think maybe you'd better have someone go out there and bring him in."

"You didn't bury him?"

"I couldn't," Clint said. "The ground was too hard. Besides, he might have some family and they'll want to bury him."

Sheriff Bennett looked down at his desk top and frowned again.

"I suppose I can have my deputy go out and get him," he said. "Once he's brought into town somebody ought to be able to identify him."

"That's fine," Clint said.

"How long you stayin' in town?" Bennett asked.

"I don't know," Clint said. "A day, maybe two."

"I'd like you to stay, at least until I get a look at that body, and until I talk with Ned Holt. You can do that, can't you?"

"I suppose I can," Clint said. Bringing the body in and talking to Holt probably wouldn't take any longer than a day or two anyway. There was no harm in agreeing to the sheriff's request.

"All right, Sheriff," Clint said. "I'll be around."

"Stay at the Molasses House hotel," Bennett

said. "It's the better of our two hotels."

"Thanks for the suggestion," Clint said.

"I'll be in touch."

"I'll be checking in on Ned Holt after I get my horses taken care of and check into the hotel," Clint said. "Maybe I'll see you there."

"Okay," Bennett said.

Sheriff Horace Bennett was making no effort to get up from behind the desk, but how fast he did or didn't move to collect that body or talk to Holt wasn't Clint's business.

"Thanks for comin' in," Bennett said.

Clint left the office, mounted Duke, and rode him back to the rig. From there he climbed aboard the rig and started looking for the livery stable. It wasn't until he was directing his team down the main street that he realized the sheriff had never answered his question about trouble with a wolf.

# FIVE

Clint put up his rig, team, and Duke at the Molasses livery stable and then walked over to the Molasses House hotel. As he entered with his saddlebags over his left shoulder and his rifle in his right hand, he saw that the clerk behind the desk looked a little familiar. He was a heavy man in his early forties, clean shaven, but if you had put a beard and mustache on him he would have been a dead ringer for the sheriff.

"Howdy," the clerk said as Clint approached the desk. "What can I do for you?"

"I need a room."

"Sure," the man said. "For how long?"

"A day, maybe two."

"Sure," the man said again. "Just sign the register please."

Clint signed in, and the clerk handed him a key.

"Just go to the head of the stairs," he said. "Need someone to help you?"

17

"No," Clint said, "I can get there on my own pretty well."

"Enjoy your stay."

He started away from the desk, but then he just had to ask.

"Excuse me."

"Yes?" the clerk said.

"Can I ask you your name?"

"Sure," the man said. "The name's Henry, Henry Bennett. If there's anything you need, just ask for me."

"Bennett," Clint said. "Would you by any chance be related to the sheriff?"

"Horace?" the man said with a big smile. "Oh yeah, Horace is my little brother." The man laughed and added, "Course you wouldn't know that to look at him, would you? Little, I mean."

"No," Clint agreed, "you wouldn't."

Little was not a word that would easily apply to either of the Bennett brothers.

"Thanks for the room."

"Sure."

Clint went up to the room to leave his saddlebags and rifle, then came back downstairs again. Henry Bennett beamed at him and continued to smile until Clint was out of the hotel. The only thing the Bennett boys didn't seem to have in common were their expressions. Horace always seemed to be frowning, while Henry appeared to smile all the time.

Clint headed for the doctor's office.

•  •  •

As Clint left the hotel Sheriff Horace Bennett appeared from behind the front desk.

"Jesus," Henry Bennett said, "you scared the livin'—Horace, ain't I asked you not to use the back door?"

"That man who just checked in . . ." Horace said, ignoring his brother's chastisement.

"Mr. Adams? What about him?"

"What did he say?"

"Nothing," Henry said. "He asked for a room."

"And?"

"And he asked me my name and if we was brothers."

"And?"

"And nothing," Henry said. "Horace, what's wrong with you?"

"He didn't say anything about a . . . wolf?"

"A wolf?"

"Keep your voice down!" Horace Bennett hissed.

Henry lowered his voice and asked, "Why would he say anything about a wolf?"

"He found a dead man outside of town, looked to be killed by a wolf."

"Oh, no," Henry said in horror. "Who was it?"

"I don't know," Horace said. "I'm sending Delbert out to fetch him. He also brought in Ned Holt."

"Ned?" Henry repeated. "What happened to him?"

"He didn't know," Horace said. "He said Ned was hurt, but he didn't see no marks on him."

"No marks?"

"That's right."

"You don't think—"

"I ain't thinkin' nothin', Brother," Horace said. He stabbed his forefinger at his brother's chest and said, "Just don't say nothin' if he starts askin' about a wolf. Understand?"

"Of course I understand, Horace," Henry said, brushing his brother's finger away. "I'm not stupid, you know."

"No," Horace said, "that's right, I forgot. I'm the stupid one."

"Horace," Henry said, "I never said—"

"Just keep your mouth shut, Henry," Horace told him. "I'm gonna tell Ned's family what happened, and then I'll be going over to the doctor's office to see about Ned's . . . injuries."

"If there are any," Henry said.

"Right," Horace said, "if there are any."

"Let me know, huh?" Henry said.

Horace ignored his brother and went back through the curtain behind the front desk.

"Aw, Horace," Henry said helplessly, "use the front. . . ."

# SIX

When Clint entered the doctor's office, Doc Craddock was just coming out of his examining room.

"Doc," Clint said, "how is he?"

Craddock looked at Clint, and instead of answering the question, he asked, "Did you talk to the sheriff?"

"I did."

"Is he notifying Ned's family?"

"He said he was."

Craddock made a face.

"Knowing Bennett, it could take hours."

"How is Holt, Doctor?"

Craddock fixed Clint with a long look and then said, "He hasn't got a mark on him, just like all the other times."

"Wait a minute—what? What do you mean, all the other times ?"

"This has happened before, Mr. Adams—several times before. We've found Ned lying in the snow just the way you did, and there hasn't ever been a mark on him."

21

"I don't understand," Clint said. "What does he say happened?"

"He doesn't say," Craddock said. "He can never remember what happened, or how he came to be . . . wherever it is he's found."

"Amnesia?"

Craddock looked at Clint with some surprise. "That's not a word a lot of people know."

"I've run across it once before," Clint said. "Is that what it is?"

"It could be," Craddock said, "except that he always remembers who he is, and his wife's name and all of that. All he can't remember is how he got to be where he was found."

"I don't understand."

"No," Craddock said, "no one does, Mr. Adams . . . least of all his family. Ned's been giving his family a real trying time these past few weeks."

"And there's nothing you can do for him?"

"How can I treat him," Craddock asked helplessly, "when I can never find anything medically wrong with him?"

"I can see where that would be a problem," Clint said. "Tell me something, Doctor."

"If I can."

"Have you been having any trouble with wolves in this area?"

Craddock gave Clint a sharp look.

"Why do you ask that?"

"I saw some wolf tracks in the snow out by the dead man and again near Holt."

"We've been having trouble with a wolf,"

Craddock said. "Just one—the same one."

"Anybody ever seen it?"

"No," Craddock said.

"Then how do you know it's the same one?"

"Everyone feels it is," Craddock said. "Some of our men are hunters, and they claim that the tracks are always the same."

"The tracks that I saw are big," Clint said, "the biggest I've ever seen."

"That's the animal," Craddock said. "And you want to know something puzzling, Mr. Adams?"

"What's that, Doc?"

"That wolf started troubling us—killing livestock—just a few weeks ago—about the same time Ned started having his problem."

"And you see a connection?"

Craddock shook his head.

"I'm just stating a fact, is all," the old man said, rubbing his forehead. "I can't make that kind of a connection. Besides, what could connect a man to a beast like that?"

"I don't know."

"Neither do I."

"You said some men were hunting the wolf?"

"They were," Craddock said, "but they quit."

"Why?"

"The way I hear it, he's too smart for them. He eludes them, circles them. There's a story that they woke up one day to find the wolf's tracks in their camp—and nobody ever heard him."

"Why didn't they have a man on lookout?"

Craddock looked at Clint and said, "They did."

The two words hung in the air for a moment, and Clint decided not to pursue the matter just then. The doctor was, after all, just telling a story.

"Doc, can I see Holt?"

"Sure," Craddock said. "He's conscious. Just like all the other times, I'll keep him here until his family comes for him. It'll probably be Rachel, his sister. She's the strongest of them."

"Thanks," Clint said. "I'll only talk to him for a minute."

"I better see about getting word to Rachel," Craddock said. "The sheriff could take a long time doing it. You can stay with him as long as you want. Nearest I can tell, he's just real tired, is all. Other than that, there just ain't anything physically or medically wrong with him. It's the damnedest thing."

"I guess so," Clint said and went into the next room to talk to Ned Holt.

# SEVEN

As Clint entered the room, the man lying on
the examining table turned his head to look at
him. Now that Ned Holt had been cleaned up,
Clint could see that he was in his early thirties
and sort of slant-jawed.

"Who are you?" Ned Holt asked.

"My name's Clint Adams. I found you and
brought you into town."

The man hesitated, then asked, "Where exactly did you find me?"

"About half a mile south of town," Clint said.
"How'd you get there?"

The man looked at him for a few moments,
and just when Clint was about to decide that
he hadn't heard him, he replied.

"I don't know."

"The doctor said you're not hurt."

"I . . . don't seem to be." He looked down at
himself, as if looking for wounds again. He was
bare to the waist, and there weren't any marks
on him that Clint could see. His chest was thin,
as were his arms.

"How do you feel?"

The man frowned and then said, "Tired, I feel real . . . tired. Like I ran a long way, you know? My legs feel . . . weak."

"Well," Clint said, "at least you're not hurt."

"I'd like to sit up," Holt said.

"Can I help you?"

"Please."

Clint helped the man into a seated position. His legs were long; even though he was sitting on a high table, his feet touched the floor.

He looked at Clint and said, "I suppose the doctor has told you that this has happened before?"

"He mentioned it, yeah."

"He thinks I'm crazy."

"I don't think so," Clint said. "At least, he didn't tell me that."

"They all think I'm crazy," Holt said. "Even my own family."

"Maybe you just think—"

"The only ones who don't think I'm crazy are the Gypsies."

"The Gypsies?" Clint asked. "What Gypsies?"

Holt remained silent for a moment, staring at the floor, then looked at Clint and said, "Never mind. It doesn't matter."

"Ned—"

"Is my family coming to get me?" Holt asked. "My sister?"

"The doctor and the sheriff both said they'd send someone to get them."

Ned Holt ran a long-fingered hand through

his thick black hair, then grabbed ahold and held on.

"It's taking her a while to get here," he said. "A while . . ."

"Why don't you just lie down and get some rest until she does get here, Ned?"

"Rest?"

"Yeah," Clint said. "You need it, remember? Your legs are weak."

"Yeah," Holt said. He released his hair and started rubbing his legs. "Yeah, they are."

"Come on," Clint said, "lie down. I'll leave you alone so you can rest."

He got the man to lie back down on the table and then headed for the door.

"Mr. Adams?" Ned called.

"Yeah?"

Ned was looking at him from his position on his back, and Clint found himself tilting his head to attempt to look directly into the man's eyes.

"Did you see anything out there?"

"See anything?" Clint repeated. "Like what, Ned?"

"I don't know," Ned said, shrugging his bony shoulders. "Anything?"

Clint wasn't sure if he should tell Holt about the dead man. In fact, he wasn't sure if he'd already told him, but he decided not to bring it up now.

"I didn't see much, Ned."

"What did you see?" Ned asked. "Tell me. It's very important."

"Well . . . I saw some tracks."

"What kind of tracks?"

Clint hesitated, then said, "They looked like wolf tracks to me."

Ned closed his eyes, and when he opened them, there was a funny look in them . . . a *haunted* look.

"Did you see . . . a wolf?"

"No," Clint said. "I never saw a wolf, just the tracks."

"I see."

Clint waited, and when nothing else was forthcoming, he said, "Anything else, Ned?"

"No," the man said, "nothing else. Thank you."

"Sure."

"For everything," Ned added.

Clint looked at the man, said, "Sure," again, and walked out.

# EIGHT

The doctor was in the office when Clint came out, making him wonder if the man had ever left. With him was Sheriff Bennett.

"Well," Bennett was saying, "I guess if it's the same as the other times I really don't have to talk to him, do I?"

"I guess not, Sheriff," the doc said.

"Hello, Adams," Bennett said. "I guess by now you heard that Ned is pretty crazy."

"No, Sheriff," Clint said, "I haven't heard that. I just talked to him, and he doesn't seem crazy to me."

"Well," Bennett said, "you just don't know him like we do."

"Who is *we*, Sheriff?" Craddock asked.

"I, uh, was talkin' about the town, Doc," Bennett said. "Just the town."

"Just don't be lumping you and me together, Sheriff," Craddock said.

"Uh, sure, Doc, sure."

"Did you notify the family yet?" Clint asked.

"I sent someone over," Craddock said before Bennett could answer.

"I was gonna do that," the lawman said. There was almost a pout in his voice.

"Yes," the doctor said, "but who knows when?"

"Aw, Doc—"

"What about the dead man?" Clint asked.

"What about him?" Bennett said.

"Did you send someone out to get him yet?"

"I don't see why I have to answer to you—" Bennett started, but the doctor cut him off.

"He's just asking a question, Horace," Craddock said. "Did someone go out to get the body yet?"

"Yeah," Bennett said reluctantly, "I sent my deputy out to get him with a buckboard."

"Delbert?" the doctor asked.

"That's right."

"Jesus," Craddock said, "he'll be back by tomorrow if he doesn't get lost."

"Never you mind, Doc," Bennett said. "Delbert won't get lost."

"When he gets back with the body, let me have a look at it."

"Adams, here, says it was tore apart by a wolf," Bennett said in a derisive tone.

"That right?" Craddock asked Clint.

"By some kind of animal," Clint said. "Could have been a wolf."

"We keeping this to ourselves, Horace?"

"Yeah, we are, Doc."

"Good."

"Doc—"

"Why don't you go make your rounds or something, Horace?" Craddock said. "I've got my work to do."

"Yeah, Doc," Bennett said, "so do I."

He backed toward the door, then turned and went outside.

"You don't like him much, do you?" Clint asked.

"What's to like?"

"You told me he was good at his job."

"I said he was good enough," Craddock said. "He does his job, but just barely, and at his own pace, which ain't much faster than a snail."

"What did he mean about keeping this wolf thing quiet?" Clint asked. "Are there people in town who don't know about it?"

"The town fathers here don't want it to get out that we're having a problem," Craddock said. "They say it will be bad for the development of the town."

"Well," Clint said, "I don't know that I'd like to argue that point."

"I'm past arguing with those people," Craddock said. He made a disgusted noise and added, "Politicians!" like it was a dirty word.

"How long do you figure it'll take Ned's family to get here for him, Doc?" Clint asked.

"A few hours."

"Time enough for me to get a beer and a steak and come back?"

"Plenty of time for that."

"Care to join me?"

"It's tempting," Craddock said, rubbing his

hand over his mouth. He had a couple of days'
beard stubble, and that plus the dryness of
his skin made a loud scratching sound. "But
I better stay here with Ned, plus I still got a
couple of hours of office time left."

"Okay, then," Clint said. "I'll be back after
I eat."

"Why?"

"What?"

"Why are you coming back?" Craddock asked.
"You did your good deed. You found him and
brought him in. Why come back?"

"I'm curious, that's all," Clint said. "I want to
make sure he's all right."

"I'd like to think he will be," Craddock said
defensively, as if Clint were impugning his
medical skills.

"Doc, you got any objection to me coming
back?"

"Me?" Craddock said. "Hell, no, I got no
objection."

"You think the family will object to my being
here?" he asked.

"Seeing as how the family we're talking
about is likely to be his sister Rachel, I doubt
she'll mind. She'll probably thank you for your
help."

"Well, that's fine, then," Clint said. "I'll have
some dinner and come on back."

"Come ahead," Craddock said. "I'll be here,
and Rachel will probably need some help getting him out to her buggy—maybe even getting

him home. You willing to go that far for your
curiosity?"

"Why not?"

"Why not?" Craddock repeated. "You ain't
heard anything about Rachel, have you?"

"No," Clint said, "only that she's his sister.
Why?"

"Just wondering," Craddock said. "Rachel's a
beauty. Thought you might have heard that,
and maybe that's what you were so curious
about."

"Nope," Clint said, "I hadn't heard that, but
thanks for telling me. Now I'll make sure I
come back and get a look at her."

"You come ahead, then," Craddock said. "If
all you get out of this is a look at Rachel Holt,
it'll be a treat for you."

"I'll look forward to it. Where's the best place
to get a steak, Doc?"

"Where are you staying?"

"The Molasses House."

The doctor made a face.

"Why there?"

"The sheriff recommended it," Clint said.
"I didn't know then that his brother worked
there."

"Worked hell," Craddock said. "Henry owns
the damned place."

"So how is it?"

"A bed's a bed," Craddock said, "just don't
try eating there. Go to the Silver Nickel Café.
Food's the best in town."

"You, uh, wouldn't have any relatives working there, would you?"

"No," Craddock said, "that's just where I go
for my meals."

"Guess that's as good a recommendation as
any, Doc," Clint said. "Thanks. See you later."

The doctor grunted something, and Clint left.
Outside he realized he hadn't asked directions
to the Silver Nickel Café. Rather than go back
in, though, he decided just to stop someone on
the street and ask them.

# NINE

The steak at the Silver Nickel was just fine, as were the vegetables that went with it. Also, the coffee was just the way Clint liked it, strong, hot, and black. When he'd told the fiftyish waitress that Doc Craddock had sent him over, she had smiled broadly and shown him to a table, promising him the best meal he'd had in a month of Sundays.

"Any friend of Doc's is welcome here," she told him. She said her name was Lois.

He didn't bother telling her that he and Doc Craddock weren't exactly friends. He didn't want to threaten his meal.

After the meal she asked him how he had liked it, and he promised to tell the doc that they had treated him real fine while he was there.

"Doc Craddock," she said, "he saved my boy's life, and then my husband's. We owe him a lot."

She tried to tell Clint that the meal was on
the house, but he insisted on paying.

"If you need Doc again, you'll need money to
pay him," he told her.

She smiled at him and took the money.

Craddock seemed a gruff man, but Lois and
her family obviously thought a lot of him. Clint
wondered if the rest of the town felt the same
way.

He left the café and headed back to the doctor's office.

Horace Bennett entered the mayor's office
with his hat in his hand.

"What's on your mind, Horace?" Mayor Eugene Masters asked. "I've got a lot of work to
do."

"I know that," Bennett said. "I just thought
you should know that Ned Holt is up to his old
tricks again."

Masters looked up from what he was writing
and gave Bennett an annoyed look. He was in
his late forties, with slate-gray hair and eyes to
match. He had been Mayor of Molasses for the
past seven years and was ready to move on to
bigger and better things politically. He didn't
need crazy men or rumors about wolf packs at
this time in his life.

"So what?" he asked.

"Well," Bennett said, "there's a stranger in
town who found him . . ." He went on to tell the
mayor about Clint Adams not only finding Ned
Holt, but a dead man as well.

"Do we know yet who the dead man is?"

"No," Bennett said. "My deputy's bringing the body in pretty soon."

"Delbert?"

"He's the only deputy I got," Bennett said. "We can't afford another one, remember?"

"Okay, okay," Masters said, holding his hands up, "never mind that. Do we know how this man was killed?"

"Adams thinks it was a wolf."

"Jesus!" Masters exploded. He was holding a pencil, and he threw it down with such force that it bounced off the desk halfway across the room. "I don't need this now, Horace. The town doesn't need it."

"I know."

"Who has this Adams talked to?"

"Doc Craddock, Ned Holt, I guess," Bennett said. "Pretty soon to Ned's sister, Rachel."

"Ah," Masters sighed, "Rachel."

Like the other men in town, Eugene fancied himself in love with Rachel Holt. It was too bad she had a crazy brother. She'd make a fine first lady, if not for that.

"All right, Horace," Masters said, "you know what has to be done. We have to keep a lid on this."

"I know."

"Then do it," Masters said, "and keep me informed."

"Yes, sir."

Bennett turned to leave, but suddenly Masters called his name.

"Horace!"

"Yeah?"

"Did you say . . . *Clint Adams?*"

"That's right."

"*The Gunsmith?*"

Bennett hesitated, then said, "Jeez, I guess so. . . ."

"Jesus . . ." Masters said, shaking his head.

# TEN

When Clint opened the door to the doctor's office and stepped in, Craddock was sitting there talking to a woman. As the door opened she stood up and turned to face him, and Clint saw why Sheriff Bennett had had a dreamy look in his eyes and what Craddock had meant when he said she was a beauty.

The doctor had not been exaggerating. Rachel Holt was a tall woman, nearly five eight or nine, full-bodied and red-haired. The red hair surprised Clint because her brother Ned was so dark. She had an oval face with full, pouty lips and sparkling green eyes.

"Rachel," Craddock said, also standing, "this fella is Clint Adams, the man who brought your brother in."

"Mr. Adams," she said, extending her hand, "I'm very grateful for what you did for my brother."

Clint took her hand and said, "It was nothing. Anyone would have done the same."

She laughed bitterly and said, "Oh, you're wrong there. There aren't that many people in this town who would have done it. You see, they all think my brother is crazy."

Clint realized he was still holding her hand and released it.

"He doesn't seem crazy to me."

"You haven't known him that long."

Clint frowned.

"Do *you* think your brother is crazy, Miss Holt?"

She took a deep breath and then let it out in a rush.

"To be honest, I don't know what to think, Mr. Adams," she said, and he admired her honesty.

She turned to Craddock and asked, "Can I take him home now, Doc?"

"Sure, Rachel," Craddock said. "There's nothing keeping him here."

"Can I help?" Clint asked.

She looked at him and said, "I think you've done enough—"

"If I can help further," Clint said, "it would be my pleasure."

"Well . . . thank you," she said. "I will need help getting him into the buggy."

"And at the other end?"

"Oh no," she said, "I couldn't ask—"

"All I have to do is saddle my horse, Miss Holt. If you can wait that long, I'll be glad to ride home with you and help get him into the house."

She hesitated a moment, then said, "I don't know what to say—uh, thank you, Mr. Adams. That's . . . extraordinarily kind of you."

"It's no trouble," he said. "I'll saddle my horse and come back for the two of you."

"Very well," she said. "Thank you, again."

"Sit down, Rachel," Craddock invited. "When Mr. Adams returns, he'll help you get your brother into the buggy."

"I won't be long," Clint said.

He left and carried a picture of Rachel Holt with him in his mind to the livery.

By the time Clint returned, Ned Holt was dressed and ready to go.

"Mr. Adams will help you to the buggy, Ned," Rachel told her brother.

"I can walk," Ned insisted, but he took only one step before his legs gave out under him.

Clint supported him beneath his right arm and walked him out to the buggy. Once he had him in the seat, he went around to the other side and helped Rachel Holt climb up. He held her by the arm and found her to be a firmly built woman.

That done, he mounted up and rode up alongside the buggy.

"You coming with us?" Ned asked.

"If you don't mind," Clint said. "I'll help get you into the house."

"Sure, why not?" Ned said.

"Thanks for everything, Doc," Rachel Holt called out to the old man.

"I wish I could do more, Rachel."

Clint glanced at the medical man's face and saw a misty-eyed look he hadn't noticed before. Was it possible that the old man was also in love with Rachel Holt?

Why not? After all, he was old, not dead.

After Clint and the Holts left, Horace Bennett returned to Doc Craddock's office.

"Delbert get back with the body?" Craddock asked.

"Not yet," Bennett said.

"What do you want, then?"

"I want to know what you told Adams."

"About what?"

"You know about what, Doc."

"Oh," Craddock said, shaking his head, "you mean about . . . wolves?"

"No," Bennett said, "I mean about a *wolf*— one wolf."

"Mr. Adams and I didn't discuss the matter, Horace," Craddock said.

"Why not?"

"It didn't come up," the doctor said, "not even after you mentioned it in front of him."

"Me?" Bennett said. "What did I say?"

"You said we had to keep this to ourselves," Craddock reminded him. "I'm sure Mr. Adams is wondering why."

"Shit," Bennett said, biting his lip.

"Yeah," Craddock said, "shit. Stop worrying about what I say and worry about what you say, Horace."

"Never mind, Doc," Bennett said. "Just make sure you don't talk to him about it. The mayor wouldn't like it, you know."

"Horace," Craddock said, "you can kiss one of my ass cheeks, and the mayor can kiss the other one. That plain enough for you?"

"Doc . . ." Horace Bennett began, and then he turned and left the office, shaking his head.

After Sheriff Bennett left, Thaddeus Craddock sat down at his desk and rubbed his hands over his face. It made such a scratching noise that he stared down at his dry hands. He must have looked like shit when Rachel Holt came into his office.

How long would it be, he wondered, before even Ned Holt's beautiful sister's limitless patience ran out? What would happen to Ned then?

Adams had asked him if there was a connection between Ned Holt and the wolf. Craddock would never admit it to anyone, but he was of the opinion that it was . . . possible.

How, he didn't know. Maybe the Gypsies knew. All he knew was that *anything* was possible.

Anything.

# ELEVEN

The ride to the Holt home was uneventful. When they reached it, Clint realized that it was more a farm than a ranch, although it didn't look like a working farm.

He exchanged very few words with Rachel Holt, but they did exchange more than a few glances, all of which went unnoticed by her brother.

When they reached the house, the front door opened and a woman came running out. Obviously, she had been watching for them. This was, he assumed, Ned Holt's wife.

"Ned," she said, running to the buggy.

Ned reached down and took his wife's hands.

"I'm fine, Libby," he said soothingly.

Rachel stepped down from the buggy gracefully before Clint could dismount and help. She walked around the buggy so that she was standing next to her sister-in-law.

"He's all right, Libby," Rachel said. "It was just like the other times."

"Oh, Ned . . ." Libby Holt said.

Clint had dismounted by this time and walked over to the buggy.

"Libby, this is Clint Adams," Rachel said. "He's the man who found Ned and brought him into town. He also helped me bring him here, and he'll take Ned into the house."

Libby Holt turned to Clint. She was a slender woman, pale, with hair just about a shade too dark to be called blond, but he didn't know what else to call it. She reached out and took one of his hands in hers. Her fingers were spidery thin, and she didn't exhibit much strength when she squeezed his hand. She was much shorter than her sister-in-law, probably less than five feet tall. She did not look like a well woman to Clint.

"I don't know how to thank you," she said, her eyes filled with emotion.

"It's all right—"

"Invite him to dinner," Ned Holt said. His voice was so low that none of them heard him very clearly.

"What?" Rachel asked.

Ned raised his voice and said, "Invite him to stay for dinner. That's better than him riding back to town right away."

"Of course," Libby said, still holding Clint's hand in hers, "of course you'll stay for dinner."

"I don't—"

"Of course he will," Rachel Holt said, giving Clint a steady, level stare over her sister-in-law's head.

"Of course," Clint said then. He looked at

Libby and said, "Thank you."

"Let's get Ned inside," Rachel said.

"I can walk," Ned said, and this time he was right. Although Clint helped him down from the buggy, he walked into the house with only his wife's arm around him. Given the amount of strength she had, that was as good as walking on his own.

"If you show me where to take them," Clint said to Rachel, "I'll unhitch the team and take care of them and the buggy."

She hesitated, then said, "There's a shack in the back. We had a barn, but that was a long time ago. It burned down. We keep the team in the shack and the buggy right alongside it. There might be room for your horse in the shack too."

"All right."

"We'll probably eat as soon as you're finished," she said. "There's a barrel of water next to the shed. You can wash up there."

"Okay," he said. "Thanks. I guess I'll see you inside, then."

"Yes," she said awkwardly, "inside."

She turned and went into the house. Clint recognized the awkwardness that was between them. They were attracted to each other and not sure what to do about it. He knew what he wanted to do about it, but he was going to have to wait for Rachel Holt to make up her mind as well.

He took the team and Duke around to the back of the house.

# TWELVE

Clint unhitched the team and walked them into the shack, then unsaddled Duke and did the same. He rubbed the team horses down, and then took longer to take care of Duke. While he was working on the big gelding, he became aware of another presence. He turned and saw a small towheaded boy watching him from the doorway.

The boy looked to be about eight, and while he was looking Clint over from Stetson to spurs, his eyes were mostly drawn to the Colt on the Gunsmith's hip.

"Hello," Clint said.

"Hi," the boy said. There was no trace of timidness in his voice or his expression.

"What's your name?"

"Tad."

"Tad," Clint said, "is Ned your father?"

The boy nodded.

"That'd make Libby your mother, then."

"Course."

"And Rachel?"

47

"My aunt."

"Anyone else in the family?"

The boy made a face.

"My sister," he said. "She's real small."

"How small?"

"She's still suckin' from the teat," Tad said, surprising Clint.

"Is that a fact?"

"Yeah," Tad said, "it's real disgustin'."

"How old are you, Tad?"

"Nine."

"Do you have chores to do around here?"

"Yup."

"Are they done?"

"Yup."

"So you're just going to watch me for a while? Is that it?"

"Yup."

"Well," Clint said, "I guess since your chores are done, there's no harm in you watching me while I do mine."

"Do you kill people?"

Clint hesitated, then said, "What?"

"You wear a gun," Tad said. "Guns are for killin' people."

"Who told you that?"

"Momma."

"Well," Clint said, continuing to brush Duke as he spoke, "it's true guns have been used to kill people, but they're also used to hunt food and . . . and to defend yourself."

"Both of them's killin'."

"Well," Clint said, "one is killing, but that's

animals. Uh, game, you know? For meat?"

"I know," the boy said. "I got a rifle to hunt rabbits with."

"Then you understand," Clint said. "Guns can kill men, but that's not what they're for."

"Have you?"

"Have I what?"

"Ever killed anybody?"

"You're single-minded, ain't you, boy?"

The boy scratched his nose. Up to that point his hands had been held behind his back. He finished satisfying the itch on his nose with his right hand and then again put it behind his back with the left.

"That's what Momma says."

"Well, your momma's right."

"So?"

"So what?" Clint asked over his shoulder. He finished with Duke and discarded the brush.

"So have you?"

Clint heaved a sigh and turned to look at the boy.

"Killed a man, you mean."

Tad nodded.

"Well, Tad, yes, I have."

"A lot of men?"

"A few."

"Why?"

"Well, like I told you before," Clint said, feeding the horses as he did, "sometimes a man has to protect himself."

"And that's what you did?"

"That's what I did, yes."

"How does it feel?" Tad asked.

"Boy, you've got more questions—" Clint said, then stopped and decided to answer. "It felt awful, that's how it felt. It felt like I killed a little bit of me too."

Tad made a face and said, "That sounds bad."

"It is, Tad," Clint said. He walked to the boy and put his hand on his shoulder. "It's real bad. Have you washed up for dinner yet?"

"Nope."

"Well, your aunt told me there's a barrel of water out here," Clint said. "Why don't we go and wash our hands together, huh?"

The boy thought that over and then nodded and said, "Okay."

"Okay," Clint said, patting his head, "come on, then. Show me where that barrel is."

# THIRTEEN

They had set an extra chair for dinner, but there was plenty of food to go around. The house on the inside was as modest as it was outside, but it was functional. Everything was there that a person would need to live, much of it handmade. As it turned out, Ned Holt made his living with his hands.

"Ned can build anything, Mr. Adams," Libby said proudly, "anything at all. He built this table that we're eating on and the benches we're sitting on."

"Nice work," Clint said, and it was. The table was sturdy, as were the benches. There was one bench on each side. Libby was sitting next to her husband, who was across from Clint. Next to Clint was Tad, who was seated between Clint and his Aunt Rachel. The baby was off to one side, in a cradle that had been built by Ned Holt.

The dinner was venison, which Ned had apparently shot himself. There were also some vegetables, which obviously had come from the

51

garden Clint had seen out behind the house.

"I went with Poppa to shoot the deer," Tad said. "Didn't I, Poppa?"

"That's right, Tad," Ned Holt said, smiling at his son fondly, "you surely did."

"But Poppa shot him," Tad said. "I was too slow."

"It's not who shoots the fastest, Tad," Clint said to the boy, "but who shoots the straightest."

"I'm a good shot, ain't I, Poppa?"

"Aren't I," Rachel Holt corrected her nephew.

"Aren't," Tad said, hanging his head. "Sorry, ma'am."

They told Clint that Rachel took care of Tad's education; she had been a schoolteacher back East before coming west to live with them.

"What about here?" Clint asked her. "Don't they have need of a schoolteacher?"

"They already had one when I arrived," Rachel said.

"Rachel's a very good teacher too," Libby said. "Better than that old Mr. Pritchard. That's why we keep Tad home now so he can learn from Rachel."

"Aunt Rachel is a real good teacher," Tad said enthusiastically.

"Thank you, Tad," she said and leaned over to bestow a kiss on the boy's head.

After dinner Libby and Rachel cleared the table, and Tad went outside to take care of some after dinner chores. Clint and Ned remained at the table with a pot of coffee between them.

"We haven't had much of a chance to talk, Ned," Clint said.

"No, we haven't."

"I feel like I know the rest of your family better than I know you."

Ned smiled a half smile and said, "They're more interesting."

"Is that right?" Clint asked. "I understood that you were real interesting."

"My blackouts, you mean?"

"Blackouts?"

"That's what Doc Craddock calls them," Ned said. "He says I black out, but I don't pass out. He thinks maybe I'm . . . doing things during those dark spells that I don't remember later."

"Things?" Clint said. "What kinds of things?"

"Do we have to talk about that now?" Libby Holt asked. "I don't want to talk about that now."

Ned looked at his wife and smiled.

"All right, Libby," he said, "we'll talk about it later." He looked at Clint and said, "We'll talk about something else now."

"All right," Clint said.

They talked about Ned's skill with his hands, his ability to do things with wood that Clint found to be amazing.

Tad came back in while they were talking and sat down next to Clint.

"Poppa could make a totem pole if he wanted to," he said proudly.

"He could?" Clint asked. "That's wonderful."

"Lemme show you somethin' he made for me," Tad said. He looked at his father and added, "Can I, please?"

"Sure, Tad."

The boy ran off into another room—there were three in the house—and came back with something that his father had made for him out of wood. He handed it to Clint, who saw that it was a flute.

"The handiwork here is incredible," he said, admiring the instrument.

"I can't play it yet," Tad said, "but someday I will, right, Poppa?"

"Yes, you will, Son."

"And you'll play it real well too," Clint said, handing it back.

"I think I'd like to get some air," Rachel Holt announced. "Clint, would you like to take a walk?"

"Sure, Rachel," Clint said. "It would be my pleasure."

"We'll be back shortly," Rachel said to her brother and sister-in-law.

"Rachel," Libby said, "I think Clint should spend the night. Will you talk him into it?"

"I'll try, Libby," Rachel said, giving Clint a look, "I'll try my best."

# FOURTEEN

Outside Rachel led him away from the house before she started talking.

"How much do you know about my brother?" she asked.

"Not much," Clint said. "I guess you could say we met when I found him, but we didn't really do much more than exchange names."

"He didn't talk to you about . . . wolves?" she asked him.

He stopped walking. She took a few more steps before she realized he wasn't walking with her anymore.

"I know that there's a problem with a wolf in the area, Rachel," he said, "but nobody had told me anything about it, other than that it's killed some livestock."

"It has," she said.

"Any of yours?"

"No."

"Rachel," Clint said, "what do you want to tell me? Or ask me?"

"Clint," she said, coming toward him, "I rec-

ognized your name when we met. I know who
you are."

"So?" He asked. "I'm not hiding from anyone."

"We need your help."

"To do what?"

"That wolf," she said, "it has to be killed."

"I heard there were some hunters after it
already," he said.

She shook her head.

"They didn't catch it, and now everyone is
afraid to go out after it."

"Why?"

"Because . . . they say it's intelligent."

"Intelligent?"

She nodded.

"Smarter than a man."

"Rachel—"

"I'm just telling you what they're saying," she
said, cutting him off. "I'm not saying I believe
it."

"What do you believe, then?"

She turned away from him and folded her
arms across her chest as if she were cold—and
maybe she was. He was starting to feel the cold
himself.

"Rachel . . ."

"My brother began to have these . . . spells,
or whatever you call them, just about the time
that wolf showed up."

"So what's that mean?"

"I think there may be a . . . a connection."

The doctor had implied the same thing.

"What kind of connection, Rachel?"

"I don't know," she said. "Something . . . unnatural."

"Have you talked to your brother about it?"

"Yes."

"And what does he say?"

"He . . . he talked to the Gypsies that are camped east of town."

"Gypsies?"

He'd heard something about them before, hadn't he?

"What do they have to do with this?"

"They told my brother some wild stories."

"What kind of wild stories?"

She turned and looked at him, then looked away, still hugging herself.

"About a wolf who walks like a man."

Clint hesitated, not sure that he had heard her right at first.

"What?"

"I know," she said, "it's crazy, but they told Ned the story and he believes it."

"That there's a wolf that walks like a man?"

"Well . . ." she said hesitantly, "there's more to it than that."

"I can't wait to hear it."

"Clint," she asked slowly, "have you ever heard of a werewolf?"

# FIFTEEN

"A were . . . what?"

"Wolf," Rachel said. "Isn't that what we're talking about?"

"Rachel," Clint said, "at this point I don't know *what* we're talking about. What the hell is a werewolf?"

"Well, as near as I can figure," she said slowly, "it's a man who turns into a wolf."

"A wolf that walks like a man?"

"Right."

"And you believe this?"

"I told you I don't," she said.

"But Ned does?"

"I think so."

"Let me get this straight. Ned thinks that during his spells . . . his spells . . . he turns into a wolf that walks like a man?"

"I think that's what he believes, Clint," Rachel said, "yes."

Clint stared at her. For the moment he was having trouble separating what she believed from what her brother believed. By virtue of

the fact that she was even talking about something so unbelievable, he found himself staring
at her in wonder.

"You're looking at me like I'm crazy."

"I don't think you're crazy, Rachel," he said.
"I think you're worried."

"I am worried," she said. "My brother thinks
he's a . . . a werewolf, a wolf that walks like
a man . . . or whatever it is. Wouldn't you be
worried?"

"Yes, I would be," Clint said. "I'd be very
worried, and I'd take him to a doctor."

"Doc Craddock says he can't find anything
wrong with Ned."

"Then take him to another doctor."

"There is no other doctor in the county."

"Then take him somewhere else, Rachel,"
Clint said. "Take him to Denver, or San Fran-
cisco, where there are doctors who know new
methods."

"That takes money," she said, folding her
arms, "and we don't have any money."

"Rachel—"

"I want your help, Clint."

"You want me to loan you money?"

"No," she said, shaking her head violently,
"not that. I wouldn't ask that."

"Then what?"

"Stay with us," she said. "Watch Ned, keep
an eye on him. When he . . . has another spell,
maybe you'll be there and you can see what
happens."

"What will that accomplish?"

"If nothing else," she said, "you'll be able to tell him that he is not a wolf that walks like a man."

"Would he believe me?"

"Yes," she said. "You're a stranger. What would you have to gain by lying to him? Yes, I think he would believe you."

Clint stroked his jaw and thought. In spite of himself, he was curious. He had never run across anything like this before. A man who thought he turned into a wolf? Werewolves? He'd never heard of such things before.

And then there was Rachel Holt.

"Is that the only reason you want me to stay, Rachel?" he asked. "To help your brother?"

She stared at him a moment, then looked past him toward the house.

"No," she said, looking at him again and moving closer, "it's not the only reason, and I think you know that as well as I do, Clint Adams."

She came right up to him and kissed him on the mouth. She was tall and barely had to lift her chin to do it. The kiss was fleeting, but there was a touch of her tongue and a promise of more—much, much more.

"Will you stay?"

"Yes, Rachel," he said, taking hold of her elbows, "I'll stay."

He pulled her to him and kissed her, deeply, hungrily. When he released her, she was out of breath and her eyes were wide.

"We'd better go inside," she said.

"All right."

She started back to the house ahead of him, then turned and said, "Oh, you'll have to sleep with Tad tonight. Either that or out in the shed with the horses."

"If Tad doesn't mind, I don't," Clint said, and followed her to the house.

Tad didn't mind, and Clint found himself rolled up on the floor next to the boy's bed, listening to the child's deep, even breathing. He wished he had been able to fall asleep as quickly as the young boy. He never fell asleep that quickly anymore. Often, as he was lying down waiting to sleep, he found his mind racing with memories. A nine-year-old boy would not have that problem when he was trying to sleep.

This time, however, he wasn't concentrating on memories. He was thinking about Rachel Holt and her brother, Ned. He was wondering how a man could come to believe that he was a wolf that walked like a man.

He was wondering about the Gypsies also. He was interested enough in this concept to go and talk to them about it. After all, they seemed to be the only ones who knew about it.

# SIXTEEN

When he woke the next morning, Clint saw Tad leaning on one elbow, looking down at him from his bed.

"How long have you been awake?" Clint asked.

"A little while."

"And how long have you been watching me?"

"A little while."

Clint frowned and said, "What time is it?"

"Time to get up and do chores," Tad said.

"What about breakfast?"

"After chores."

The boy sat up and got down from his bed, deftly stepping over Clint.

"Is it light yet?" Clint asked while the boy got dressed.

"No," Tad said, "not for about a half hour."

"When does your mom cook breakfast?"

Tad turned and looked at him and said, "In a little while."

Clint rolled over and groaned. He'd slept on the ground before, so why were his muscles

aching from it this morning? The only differ-
ence between this and sleeping on the trail was
that this floor was wood. Maybe that was it.

He sat up and stretched his arms up over his
head. His gun was on the floor next to him. He
suddenly became aware that Tad was looking
at the gun.

"Why does my gun fascinate you, Tad?" he
asked, picking up the holster and holding it in
his hands.

The boy shrugged.

"I don't know."

"Does your dad have one?"

"No," Tad said, "we just have rifles."

"Then you've never seen a handgun?"

"Not up close."

"Would you like to see this one?"

The boy nodded.

"You get your mom's okay, and I'll show it to
you. How's that?"

"Great!" the boy said.

"Okay then," Clint said, "you go and do your
chores and we'll see about it."

The boy put on his boots and started for the
door, then stopped and turned.

"Mr. Adams?"

"You can call me Clint, Tad."

"Clint," Tad said, "are you gonna be staying
with us for a while?"

"For a while, yes."

"Because of Poppa?"

"What about your poppa?" Clint asked.

"Him and the wolf, I mean."

"What do you know about your father and the wolf, Tad?" Clint asked.

The boy looked at the floor.

"Come here for a second, Tad."

Tad left the door and walked over to where Clint was sitting on the floor. Clint put his gun aside and put his hands on the boy's thin shoulders.

"What do you know, Tad?"

"Poppa made me promise not to tell."

"Well, you already started to tell me, didn't you?" Clint asked.

Reluctantly, the boy nodded.

"And I am here to help your father, right?"

"Are you?" the boy asked, the look on his face an anxious one.

"Yes, I am," Clint said. "I'm going to try to help him, but to do that I have to know what's going on."

The boy hesitated, biting his bottom lip, and Clint gave him time to think.

"Tad?" he said, after a few moments.

"Poppa wants to kill the wolf."

"What wolf?"

"The one that's been killing stock around here."

"Has he seen it?"

"He says he has."

"Does he know where to find it?"

"He says he does."

"How?"

"He says . . . he says that him and the wolf think alike."

"Tad, how much do you know about your father and . . . and his spells?"

"Poppa says that when he has a spell it's because of the wolf," Tad said. "He says that if he kills the wolf, the spell will be broken."

"And who told him that?"

"The Gypsies," Tad said, "he says that the Gypsies told him."

"The Gypsies?" Clint asked. "Do you know where I can find the Gypsies, Tad?"

"Sure," the boy said. "They're camped at Wilson's Pond."

Wilson's Pond. Clint figured he wouldn't have too much trouble finding it.

"Now Tad, I want to ask you one more question and then you can go and do your chores."

"Yes, sir?"

"Did your father ever mention the name of any of these Gypsies?"

"Just one."

"And what's the name?"

"Martika," Tad said. "He said that she told him about the wolf."

"Martika."

"Yes, sir."

# SEVENTEEN

At breakfast Clint put what Tad had told him together with what Rachel had told him and came up with the location of the Gypsies. They were camped at Wilson's Pond, east of town.

"It's no secret, you know," Ned Holt said across the table.

"What's no secret, Ned?"

"Who you are, and why you're staying."

"Why don't you tell me why I'm staying, Ned," Clint said. "Let's see if we're both thinking the same thing."

"It's the wolf."

"What about it?"

"You heard about the bounty."

Clint frowned.

"What bounty?"

"A thousand dollars the ranchers around here have put on that wolf's head."

A thousand-dollar bounty? Clint hadn't heard about that until now.

"I'm gonna collect that bounty, Clint," Ned said.

"I hope you do, Ned," Clint said. "In fact, I'll even help you."

Now it was Ned's turn to frown.

"Why?" he asked. "You're the Gunsmith. You could kill that wolf anytime you wanted to. Why would you help me and let me collect the bounty?"

"Why not?"

"You're a gunman," Ned said, "you work for money."

"Ned," Clint said, planting his elbows firmly on the table, "I have never sold my gun for money, and I never will."

"But . . . your reputation—"

"Don't believe everything you hear, Ned," Clint said. "Now, about the wolf, I'm not a hunter either. You know the area, and you might have some idea of where we can find the wolf. Look, if it will make you feel any better, you can split the bounty with me."

"How?" Ned asked. "Half?"

Clint shrugged.

"I don't care," he said. "This is your home that you're protecting. You split it with me any way you want to."

Ned looked puzzled. He looked first at his sister and then at his wife. Libby nodded to him, giving him an anxious look. She didn't want her husband going after the wolf alone.

"Well, all right, then," Ned said. "When should we start?"

"Tomorrow," Clint said.

"Why tomorrow?" Ned asked. "It's still early, we can get started now."

"My gear and my rifle are in town," Clint said. "I have to go in and collect everything and check out of the hotel. I'll be back later this evening."

Grudgingly Ned said, "Oh, okay, then." He put his napkin down on the table and said, "I've got chores. I'll see you later."

Ned went out, and Rachel, who was sitting next to Clint, put her hand on his arm.

"Thanks."

"Yes," Libby said from across the room, "thank you, Clint. Rachel told me you agreed to stay and help with Ned. I'm so worried . . ."

"It'll be okay, Libby."

"Maybe killing that wolf will free Ned," Rachel said. "Maybe once that animal's dead, things will get back to normal around here."

"Maybe," Clint said, wiping his mouth. "I've got to get into town."

"I'm coming with you," Rachel said.

Clint looked at her and said, "Why?"

Beneath the table she put her hand on his thigh.

"I just need a ride," she said.

# EIGHTEEN

As it turned out, Rachel Holt had a definite use for Clint's hotel room in mind, before he gave it up.

Inside that hotel room they got to know each other a lot better.

Clint discovered that her full, firm breasts were tipped with extremely sensitive nipples. As he teased them with his lips and tongue, she shuddered in his arms and cried out. She cradled his head in her hands, pulling him more tightly to her. He ran his tongue down the valley between her breasts, savoring the taste of her salty sweat. He slid his right hand down over her belly, through the tangled bush between her legs, until he found her wet and waiting. He stroked her with his fingers until her legs quivered and she stifled a scream with the pillow.

"Oh, God . . ." she said moments later, still trying to catch her breath. Her eyes were wide, and she was blinking, as if trying to focus them. "No man has ever done that to me before. . . ."

"What a shame," he said, rubbing her belly. "You react so well to it."

"Oh, how else would I react to . . . that?" she asked. She reached between them and touched his rigid penis. "It's your turn now."

"My turn for what?" he asked.

She teasingly drew one nail along the underside of his penis, and he jumped at how sensitive it felt.

"Your turn to react," she said and slithered down between his legs to use her mouth on him. . . .

Later she mounted him, lifting her hips and taking him inside of her. She did it slowly, coming down on him, easing him into her, until at the last moment she ground herself down on him, taking him completely. She began to rock on him, then, taking her weight on her knees and moving over him in a back and forth motion. No woman had ever done this to him before, and he found himself liking it . . . a lot!

Finally, when he could hold the explosion in no longer, he gripped her buttocks tightly, pulled her to him, and let himself go. He groaned out loud as he ejaculated into her, and she closed her eyes tightly and screamed without benefit of the pillow. . . .

"God," she said later, lying in his arms, "it was as if you were scalding me."

"Did I hurt you?"

"Yes," she said, "and it was wonderful." She

reached behind her and rubbed her buttocks. "I think I'm going to have the marks of your fingers on my ass forever."

He reached around to rub her too, but she slapped his hand away.

"If you start that, we'll never get out of here," she said. "We have to get back to the house before Ned does something stupid."

"Like what?"

"Like going after that wolf alone."

"I don't think he'll do that."

"Why not?"

"Because now he's got a better chance of killing that wolf with me than without me."

"Well, I hope he knows that."

"We still have to hurry, though." He disentangled himself from her and sat up.

"Why?"

"I want to make a stop before we go back."

"A stop?" she asked as he got off the bed. "Where? What for?"

"Wilson's Pond," Clint said. "Do you know where it is, Rachel?"

"Well sure, but what's there?"

"The Gypsy camp."

"The Gypsies. Why do you want to talk to them?"

"I want to talk to a woman named Martika," Clint said. "She's the one Ned has been talking to."

"How do you know that?" She got off the bed herself and started to get dressed.

He looked at her and said, "Tad told me."

"Tad?" She looked at him in complete surprise. "What does Tad know about all of this?"

"More than you and me, apparently," Clint said. He told her what Tad had told him that morning.

"Ned's been confiding in Tad?"

"I guess so."

"But . . . why not me? Or Libby?"

"I guess he wanted to talk to a man, and Tad's the closest thing to another man in your family."

"And he told Tad about this Martika?"

"Yes."

"So that's what Ned's been doing when he has these spells?" she asked. "He's been out hunting for this wolf?"

"Maybe."

"Why do you say maybe?"

"Well," Clint said, strapping on his gun, "when I found him, he didn't have a rifle with him. Has he lost a rifle lately?"

"No," she said, "it's hanging on the wall. Why?"

"It's just that I never yet saw a man hunt for an animal *without* a rifle."

# NINETEEN

Clint decided he wanted to stop in and see the sheriff before he went to talk to the Gypsies.

"I've got no use for the sheriff," Rachel told him. "I'll wait outside."

"Suit yourself."

Clint went into the office and found the sheriff's bulk behind his desk again, just like last time.

"Adams," Horace Bennett said. "What brings you back here again? Gettin' ready to leave town, I hope?"

"As a matter of fact, I am."

"Well, good. Headin' on, eh?"

"Not really," Clint said. "I'm going to be a guest of the Holts for a few days."

"Eh? The Holts?" Bennett said, frowning. "Is Rachel gonna be there?"

"She lives there, doesn't she?"

"Well . . . well, what are ya gonna be doin' out there?" Bennett asked.

"Oh, I don't know," Clint said. "Maybe I'll do some hunting. You neglected to mention that there was a thousand-dollar bounty on that wolf, Sheriff."

"You were just passin' through," Bennett said. "Why bother you with that? Besides, the town council don't approve of that bounty. That's been put up by the ranchers in the area. Having a bounty means you're gonna have a bunch of storekeepers out there totin' guns. You know what that means, don't you?"

"Sure," Clint said, "some dead storekeepers. That kind of money, though, should probably bring in some professionals."

"Like you?"

"No," Clint said, "I mean wolfers. Seen any in town?"

"Not that I know of."

"Well," Clint said, "they'll be here."

"So that's why you're stayin'?" Bennett asked. "To go after that wolf?"

"Maybe," Clint said, "but basically I'm staying because Rachel Holt invited me."

"Rachel invited you? Herself?"

"That's right."

Bennett didn't like that, but he couldn't think of anything to say about it.

"Tell me about the Gypsies camped out at Wilson's Pond, Sheriff."

"What about them?"

"How long have they been there?"

Bennett shrugged. "A few weeks, I guess," he said. "Come to think of it, they got here just around the time that wolf did. Kind of a coincidence, huh?"

"I guess," Clint said. "Have you had any trouble with them since they got here?"

"Some, in the beginning," Bennett said. "They used to come into town for supplies, you know? And they'd start tellin' fortunes and stuff. Also, there's a black-haired gal out there that all the men in town were after."

"So what happened?"

"After a few fights I told them to stay out of town before somebody got hurt."

"And?"

"Now they come into town only for supplies, and that's just every few days. They come in two at a time, and that black-haired gal stays out at their camp."

"How long do you think they intend to stay?"

"I don't know," Bennett said. "I asked them that myself, and they don't know either. I tell you what, though. I wish they'd leave right quick. Maybe that wolf would go with them."

Clint wondered how many other people had made that connection between the Gypsies and the wolf—and with Ned Holt's spells.

"All right, Sheriff," Clint said. "I just wanted to keep you up-to-date on my movements. I might be in town from time to time."

"Long as you don't cause any trouble, I got no problem with that," the man said, but Clint knew he didn't mean it. It was eating away at Bennett that Rachel Holt had invited Clint to stay.

He started for the door, then stopped and turned.

"Tell me something," Clint said.

"What?"

"How does this black-haired Gypsy woman compare to Rachel Holt?"

He assumed that the black-haired woman would turn out to be the Martika he was looking for.

Bennett gave Clint a long, knowing look and said, "Close, very close."

If that were true, he was really looking forward to meeting Martika—and having Rachel along with him would make it that much more interesting.

Outside he found Rachel waiting for him, but his eye was caught by a man who was riding down the street.

"You know him?" Clint asked her.

Rachel looked and shook her head.

"No, why?"

"He's a wolfer."

"How can you tell?"

"Well, for one thing he's wearing some skins," Clint said. "Also, he's carrying a rifle and not wearing a side arm."

"That makes him a wolfer?"

"Well," Clint said, wrinkling his nose as the man rode by, "there's also the smell."

At that moment the odor hit Rachel, and she turned her head and touched her nose.

"My God," she said, "what is that?"

"The last thing a wolfer wants is to smell like a man," Clint said. "It tips off the wolf to his presence."

"Phew!" Rachel said. "Does he have to smell like a wolf too?"

"It's safer that way," Clint said. "For him, not the wolf."

Rachel fanned the air in front of her face and said, "He's a professional hunter, then?"

"A professional *wolf* hunter, yeah."

"Clint, I don't want to sound . . . greedy, but in addition to getting rid of the wolf for Ned's sake, we *could* use that thousand dollars."

"I know," Clint said, "but he's not the only professional that kind of bounty is going to attract. We're going to have some real competition, Rachel."

"Then maybe we better get going," she said.

"Wilson's Pond," Clint said. "Let's get my rig and head out that way. Maybe the Gypsies can give us a head start."

What Rachel didn't know was that Clint had not only recognized the wolfer for what he was, but had recognized the man personally. He had crossed paths with Vin Hacker a time or two, and the two were something less than good friends. He didn't know whether Hacker had seen him or not, but knowing the man for the sharp-eyed hunter that he was, he would have bet on it.

With Hacker on the trail of the wolf, it would be hard to bring the animal down. He hoped now that the Gypsies really could give him some sort of an edge on the professional wolf hunter.

• • •

Vin Hacker had indeed seen and recognized Clint Adams as he rode his horse down the main street of Molasses. He did not act as if he had, though. He saw no reason to. He and Adams did not like each other. Also, he saw no reason to believe that Adams was even in Molasses for the same purpose he was.

He'd be a happy man if he didn't have to deal with Adams at all.

And Clint Adams would be a lucky man.

# TWENTY

Clint had had experience with Gypsies on only one other occasion, and he had found them to be a fiery-tempered, unpredictable people. On the other hand, if they liked you, they were wonderful hosts.

On the way he asked Rachel if she knew how many Gypsies there were in the camp.

"No," she said. "I've never been there, and Ned has never talked to me about them." She said that last a little bitterly.

"Have you and your brother always been close, Rachel?" Clint asked.

"Yes," she said. "That's why it puzzles me that he hasn't been confiding in me since . . . since all of this began happening."

"Maybe he thought you'd think he was crazy," Clint said.

"He's my brother," she said quickly, "why would I . . ." Then she stopped, because she remembered that she *did* think he was crazy.

"Clint," she said, "it sounds crazy to you, right?"

"Oh yeah," Clint said, "if he really believes it, then I'd say that he's a little crazy . . . for now."

"For now?"

"Well, maybe it's temporary," Clint said. "Has he been under a lot of pressure lately?"

"Well, sure," Rachel said. "There's no money, and he hasn't been getting all that much work. Of course he's worried, but a lot of people get worried. They don't go crazy because of it."

"People react in different ways," Clint said.

"Do you think that killing that wolf will bring him back to normal?"

"I don't know, Rachel," Clint said. "There are still too many coincidences here to suit me."

"Like what?"

"Like Ned's spells, the appearance of the wolf, and the Gypsies," he said. "They all started at just around the same time. Why is that?"

"I don't know."

"Well," he said, "maybe the Gypsies can tell us. How far are we from the pond?"

"Not far," she said. "We should be there in a few minutes."

"Good," Clint said. "Maybe then we'll get some answers."

While Clint and Rachel were riding out of town, Vin Hacker reined in his horse in front of the City Hall and went inside. He jogged upstairs and knocked on the door of the mayor's office.

"Come in," Eugene Masters called out.

Hacker entered, closing the door behind him. Masters was about to speak when the man's odor hit him full force in the nose.

"Oh, God . . ."

"You sent for me, Mayor," Hacker said. It was not an apology.

"Couldn't you have bather first?" Masters asked, fanning the air in front of his face.

"You didn't call for me because I'm sweet-smelling," Hacker said. "Besides, it takes me too long after a bath to get my smell to this point, where a wolf can't tell me as a man."

"You mean you *have* bathed in the past?"

A small smile tugged at the corners of Hacker's mouth and he said, "Once or twice. You mind tellin' me why I'm here? I assume you've got a problem with a wolf?"

"Yes," Mayor Masters said, "we have a rogue wolf on our hands. It's been killing some of our stock, and we need to get rid of it before the word gets out."

"Fine," Hacker said. "Just give me some idea of what I'm looking for, and I'll get rid of it for you."

"Well, Hacker," the mayor said, "there's one or two more problems I'd like to talk to you about."

All of a sudden Vin Hacker had an idea that he and Clint Adams were going to cross paths again.

# TWENTY-ONE

"What's the other job?" Hacker asked.

"Don't sit down—" Mayor Masters started to say, but Hacker had already dropped into a chair. He stared at the mayor, daring him to say something. Instead Masters stood up and opened the window behind him, the one that overlooked the main street. A breeze wafted in, but it did little to cut into the scent of Vin Hacker.

"Clint Adams," Masters said. "Do you know him?"

"Yeah, I do."

"Personally?"

Hacker nodded.

"Even better," Masters said. "There's a fella in town named Ned Holt. Actually, he lives just outside of town. He's a problem."

"What kind of problem?"

"He's crazy," Masters said.

"In what way?"

"I . . . don't think you need to know that, Hacker," Masters said. He didn't even want

Hacker to know what Holt's real problem was. As if it wasn't bad enough they had a wolf running loose killing stock—and who knew, maybe people too—they also had a crazy man who thought he was a wolf. "Do you?" Masters asked. "I mean, to do your job?"

"Just what is my job?" Hacker asked. "And how does it involve Adams?"

"Your job is to get rid of the wolf," Masters said, "and, if possible, Ned Holt."

"I usually hunt animals," Hacker said. "To kill a man is gonna cost you extra."

"I'll pay extra, don't worry," Masters said. "That's one and two, the wolf and Holt."

"And Adams?"

"He's number three."

"How's he involved?"

"He's staying with the Holts at their house," Masters said. "He's going to be trying to help Ned Holt."

"Do what?"

Masters hesitated, then said, "Again, I don't think you need to know—"

"If you're gonna keep me in the dark, Mayor," Hacker said, interrupting the man, "it's gonna cost you even more."

"Look," Masters said, "I don't need word getting out about what's going on in this town. To keep Holt from talking—or Adams—I'll pay whatever it will take."

"What do you want done about Adams?"

"Whatever it takes to keep him quiet," Masters said. "If you have to kill him, do it. I'll pay,

Hacker. You know I can pay."

Hacker had worked for Masters a few times before, and the man was right. He *had* always paid what was owed.

"I know that."

"Then do the job," Masters said. "When it's done, come and see me and we'll settle up. Okay?"

Hacker hesitated, then said, "Sure, but I need some pocket money."

"I thought you might," Masters said. He took an envelope out of his desk and tossed it across to Hacker's side. The wolfer picked it up and tucked it away inside his skins somewhere without counting it.

Masters stared at the big wolfer—Hacker stood at least six three and was wide across the shoulders—and marveled at how, suddenly, he didn't notice the smell as much.

"Can you handle Adams?" Masters asked.

"Mayor, I can handle anybody," Hacker said, "as long as I'm paid to do it."

"Well, you'll be paid."

"Then I'll handle him," Hacker said, rising and heading for the door.

"How?" Masters asked.

At the door Hacker turned and said, "I don't think you need to know that."

After Hacker left, Masters suddenly became aware of the smell again. Funny, it seemed stronger now that the man was gone. He opened the window wide and stood in front of it for several minutes until the smell in the room became bearable again.

Hopefully, he wouldn't have to deal with that odor again until the job was done.

Outside Hacker mounted up and headed for the livery stable to board his horse. In the past when he and Adams had crossed paths they had been able to avoid going up against each other. Hacker had always wondered, though, who would come out on top if they ever did tangle.

Now, thanks to Mayor Masters and his money, it looked like he was going to find out.

# TWENTY-TWO

As Clint and Rachel came within sight of the Gypsy camp by the pond, he noticed that there were only two wagons. Off to one side about six horses were picketed. If the wagons took two horses apiece, that left two others to be ridden. That meant there'd be at least half a dozen people in the camp, maybe more, depending on how many they managed to cram into each wagon.

"Doesn't look like that many," Rachel said.

"No," Clint said, "but after the trouble they've had in town I don't know how receptive they're going to be to company, so let me do the talking, okay?"

She didn't answer.

"Rachel?"

"Sure."

Clint looked at her, but she was staring straight ahead. He was somewhat less than confident in the sincerity of her answer.

As they approached the camp, they attracted some attention. A man stepped away from one of the wagons and was joined seconds later by a woman. They both had raven-black hair and dark skin. The man was over six feet, wearing a red shirt and jeans. He had an earring in his left ear.

The woman was as tall as Rachel, maybe taller. She was full-bodied and firm, wearing a long multicolored dress and a headband to match. She had many bracelets on each wrist and big hoop earrings. Clint assumed this was the woman the sheriff had said was close to Rachel in beauty. Seeing her now, he agreed. It would be hard to choose between the two women. For most men it would probably come down to what they liked, a woman with dark hair and dark skin, or red hair and fair skin.

The man's eyes were on Rachel, inspecting her carefully as she and Clint rode closer. Being a Gypsy man who lived most of his life with dark women, he seemed to find the redheaded Rachel very interesting.

The woman was eyeing Clint with the same sort of intensity. He took a quick look at Rachel and saw that she was studying the pair closely. Clint wondered who she found more interesting, the man because he was attractive, or the woman because she was beautiful. In Clint's experience good-looking women often felt competitive—until they got to know each other better, anyway. Rachel and the Gypsy woman Martika—if that's who she was—would each see the other as a potential rival for the attention of men.

"Hello," Clint said.

"Good afternoon," the man greeted. "Why have you come here?" The man was polite, but he got right to the point. Both he and the woman were now looking directly at Clint.

"My name is Clint Adams, and this is Rachel Holt."

"Holt?" the woman asked, looking at Rachel again.

"That's right," Clint said. "I believe you know her brother, Ned?"

"We have met him," the man said. "My name is Erik, this is my sister, Martika. Again, please, why have you come here?"

"To talk to you, if we may," Clint said.

"About what?" Erik asked.

"About Ned Holt."

Erik and Martika exchanged a long glance.

"Step down, then, and join us for lunch," Erik said. "Nicholas!"

A lad of about sixteen appeared from inside one of the tents. He was tall and gangly, dark-haired like the others. He greatly resembled Erik.

"This is my son, Nicholas," Erik said. "He will see to your horses. Please, step down. You will be our guests, and we will talk."

Clint nodded, exchanged a glance with Rachel, then they dismounted and handed their horses over to Nicholas. The lad was having a hard time taking his eyes off Rachel.

"Momma?" Erik shouted.

An older woman appeared from behind one

of the wagons. She was about sixty or so, with long gray hair and dark, heavily wrinkled skin.

"Why are they here, Erik?" she demanded. She was holding a ladle in her hand, brandishing it as if it were a weapon.

"They are our guests for lunch, Momma," Erik said.

"Pah!" she said. "Guests."

"Do not mind my mother," Erik said. "She does not like company. Please, come to our fire."

Erik and Martika led the way around the wagon, where Clint saw their camp fire. There was a large pot suspended above it.

"That's all right," Clint said, "not everyone likes strangers."

"No," Erik said, "that is true. We have learned that from the treatment we received in your town."

"I'm not from town," Clint said. "I'm just passing through."

"I see," Erik said. "We, too, are passing through."

"Really?" Clint asked. "It was my understanding that you were camped here for a while."

"Yes, that is true," the man said, "but we do not intend to remain here permanently." He looked at the old woman and asked, "Is lunch ready, Momma?"

"It is ready." She was sulking.

"Then serve our guests first, then we will eat and talk."

"Do you know my brother?" Rachel asked Martika impatiently.

The black-haired woman had not said a word since Rachel and Clint had dismounted.

"I know him."

"How?"

The old woman was staring at Erik, a puzzled frown on her face.

"This is Rachel," Erik said to her. "She is Ned Holt's sister."

"Ah . . ." the old woman said, and suddenly she found Rachel very interesting. She walked up to her and stared at her intently, studying her face.

"What is she doing?" Rachel asked.

"She is looking," Erik said.

"For what?"

"Your brother has the mark," the old woman said to her. "I want to see if you have it too."

"What mark?" Rachel asked, touching her face with both hands, as if there were something on it that she would be able to feel.

The woman was too engrossed in her examination to answer.

"What mark is she talking about?" Rachel demanded from Erik and Martika.

The brother and sister exchanged another glance, and then it was Erik who spoke.

"The mark of the wolf."

# TWENTY-THREE

Over the best rabbit stew he'd ever tasted, Clint and Rachel talked to Erik and Martika about Ned Holt—but not until Rachel had gotten the business of the "mark" out of the way.

"What is the mark of the wolf?" she asked Erik after the old woman had finished her examination.

"It is an old myth," Erik said. "You should not concern yourself with it."

"Well, I do concern myself with it," she said. "You people have got my brother believing in some . . . some wolf myth—"

"Your brother has the mark," the old woman said, looking up from the pot of stew.

"There she goes again," Rachel said.

"Momma—" Erik said.

"She does not have the mark," the old woman said with a shrug. "She should be happy."

In spite of herself Rachel *did* feel a flush of relief when the old woman said that she didn't have the mark of the wolf—but then that made her angry.

91

"Listen," she said, "I want to talk to you people about my brother—"

"Sit," Erik said, "and eat, and we will talk."

"But—"

"Let's sit, Rachel," Clint said. "These people are offering us their hospitality."

"Sure," Rachel said, "and their superstitions."

"It is up to you," Erik said firmly, "which you will accept, and which you will not."

He and Rachel stared at one another steadily, and when it became clear that neither was going to speak, Clint did.

"I think for now," he said slowly, "we'll accept the hospitality."

Clint accepted the bowl of stew that Martika handed him, and when their eyes met, he thought he saw something there. Amusement? Interest? Maybe both.

"What do you want to know about your brother?" Erik asked. He had taken to speaking to Rachel rather than Clint. Clint didn't mind. It was obvious that she was not going to leave the talking to him, and when he thought about it, why should she? After all, it *was* her brother they were talking about.

"I want to know how and why you convinced him that he could turn into a wolf who walks."

Said out loud like that it sounded silly to Clint. He watched as Erik and Martika looked at each other. Their mother kept her head down and concentrated on her stew. Nicholas, the boy, was still staring at Rachel. Clint had not seen any other Gypsies around except for these four. He was still wondering if there were more. Where was the boy's mother? Was she still alive?

"A werewolf," Martika said.

"What?"

"We talked with your brother about were-wolves," Martika said, looking directly at Rachel.

"It is an old myth," Erik interjected.

"We did not," Martika went on, "tell him that he was one."

"What about these spells he's been having?" Rachel asked.

"Spells?" Erik said.

"He doesn't remember where he's been or what he's done."

Erik frowned. "Perhaps your brother should see a doctor," he said.

"He has," Rachel told him. "The doctor can't find anything medically wrong with him."

Erik shrugged.

"I am sorry," he said. "I do not know what to tell you."

"Do you people really believe in this myth?" Clint asked.

Erik looked at his mother, who was not paying any attention to the rest of them.

"Some of us do, yes," Erik said.

"Well," Rachel said, "maybe in your country you could believe, but not here—and not about my brother."

"He has the mark," the old woman said without looking up.

"Could you get her to stop saying that?" Rachel said to Erik.

"Easy, Rachel," Clint said. "Erik, do you know anything about the wolf that's roaming these parts?"

"We have heard of it, of course," Erik said, "but we know nothing of such an animal."

"It's a wolf," Rachel said insistently, "a normal, everyday, walks-on-all-fours wolf."

Erik looked at her and calmly said, "Yes."

"You haven't seen it?" Clint asked.

"No," Erik told him.

Clint looked around, then asked Erik, "Are there just the four of you here?"

The Gypsy hesitated, then said, "No, there are two others, my father and my uncle."

"Where are they?"

"Hunting," he said, then pointed to the pot on the fire and added, "for more rabbit."

"I see," Clint said. "Do you think either of them have seen this wolf?"

"They would have said so," Erik answered, "and they have not. Of course, they might have seen it while they were out today. I will not know that until they have returned."

"Naturally," Clint said, starting to get up. "Well, thank you for your hospitality. The stew was wonderful. We'll be going now."

"But—" Rachel started, but Clint didn't let her get any further.

"We have to get going, Rachel," he said, grabbing her arm and helping her to her feet.

"Nicholas," Erik said, also rising, "please, our guests' horses."

"Yes, Poppa."

As Nicholas walked their horses over, Clint was sorry he had not brought his rig from town. He felt sure that the Gypsies knew more than they were telling. He might have been able to ask them if he could camp with them—but then he wouldn't have been able to keep an eye on Ned Holt. So it was just as well he had arranged for the liveryman to watch over the rig until he was ready to leave the area.

"Thank you," he said to Nicholas.

The boy ignored Clint and gaped at Rachel, who seemed to notice it for the first time. She bestowed a smile on the boy that made him blush and look away.

Clint and Rachel mounted up and looked down at Erik and Martika.

"Please let us know how your brother is doing," Erik said. He was stroking Rachel's horse's nose and speaking directly to her again. "We are . . . interested."

I'll bet you are, Clint thought.

"If you could just tell us—" Rachel started, but Clint cut her off.

"We'll be sure to keep you informed, Erik," Clint said. "Perhaps we can come and visit you and your family again soon?"

"Please do," Martika said, looking directly at Clint. "You will always be welcome here."

Clint caught her eyes and held them. Martika's gaze was bold, steady, and Clint found it hard to look away, almost as if her black eyes had some hypnotic ability.

"Thank you, Martika."

He turned his horse and Rachel followed, although it was obvious she still had more on her mind.

Clint was sure that as soon as they were out of earshot of the camp he'd hear all about it.

# TWENTY-FOUR

"What was that all about?" Rachel demanded as soon as they were far enough away from the camp.

"They know more than they're telling us," Clint said confidently.

"Well, I knew that," she said. "Why didn't you let me ask more questions?"

"Because it didn't matter how many questions we asked," Clint said, "they weren't going to tell us more than they wanted to."

"We could have forced them."

"How?"

"Well . . . you and your gun. With your gun you could have made them—"

"I don't work that way, Rachel," he said, reining Duke in hard.

She rode past him a few feet before she got her mount stopped.

"If you think you've hired a gunman, then we'd better part company right—"

"Okay, okay," she said, "I'm sorry—Jesus, I'm *really* sorry, Clint."

He hesitated a moment, then said, "All right, forget it . . ."

"It's just that I'm so worried about Ned."

"I know," Clint said. "I have an idea."

"What?" she asked hopefully.

"Well, since the Gypsies wouldn't tell us anything about Ned and the wolf," he said, "maybe I can get Ned to tell me something about the Gypsies."

"Do you think so?"

"It's worth a try."

"Then let's go," she said.

She rode on ahead of him, and he followed behind. He was not thinking about Ned Holt, though, or his beautiful red-haired sister. Clint found himself thinking about the black-haired, black-eyed Gypsy woman, Martika. He could almost feel her eyes—those deep, black eyes—still boring into his. Clint had once seen a man claim to hypnotize another at a circus, but he had never believed in hypnosis. He thought now, however, that if anyone *could* hypnotize another person, it would have to be Martika, with those beautiful black eyes.

As soon as Clint Adams and Rachel Holt were out of earshot, Erik turned and walked to his mother.

"You should not have said anything."

She looked at him and said, "I am a queen among my people, and you are a prince. As such, we say what we feel when we feel it."

"Momma—"

"Leave her be," Martika said, putting her hand on his arm. "The damage is done, my brother."

Erik looked at Martika and then nodded.

"You are right, my sister," he said. "Now we must deal with the consequences."

"We *could* move on," she said, "leave this place."

"No," Erik said, "we cannot. The wolf is still out there. He would follow. I want to end it here, and now. I am tired of the chase."

Martika looked off into the distance and said, "They will be back."

"Yes," Erik said, "and when they return, we will be ready for them."

Martika watched her brother walk to his wagon and climb inside. She wondered about his comment. Was he tired of chasing the wolf, she wondered, or of *being* chased by it?

# TWENTY-FIVE

When Clint and Rachel returned to the Holt house, they found Ned sitting out front on the low porch with Tad. Ned held a rifle across his lap.

"Tad," Rachel said as they dismounted, "would you take care of the horses?"

"I don't know if Tad can handle Duke," Clint said frankly. "Why don't you give him your horse, and he and I will take them around back and see to them."

"All right," she said, handing the reins to Tad.

"Come on, son," Clint said.

They started around the house, and Tad was very quiet as he led his aunt's horse.

"What's wrong?"

Tad looked up at Clint.

"I asked Mom if you could show me how your gun works," he said.

"Oh?" Clint said. "And what'd she say?"

"She said no," Tad said. "She said she didn't

want me anywhere near your gun."

"Well, she's your mother, Tad," Clint said. "We have to abide by what she says. She only wants what's best for you, doesn't she?"

"Aw, she never wants me to have any fun," Tad said. "That's what moms are like."

"I guess so."

"Was your mom like that?"

"My mom?" Clint hadn't thought about his mother in years. "Yeah, that's what my mom was like, all right. Just like yours."

"All moms are the same, huh?" Tad asked.

"I guess so."

When they reached the shed, they each started unsaddling the horses.

"Clint?"

"What?"

"Could you show me anyway?"

"Tad," Clint said, "that wouldn't be right."

"Mom would never know," Tad said eagerly. "We wouldn't have to tell her."

"I couldn't do that, Tad."

"Don't you think a boy should learn how to shoot a gun?" Tad asked.

"That's a loaded question if ever I heard one, Tad," Clint replied.

"What's that mean?"

"It means that any way I answer it I could get in trouble."

"You ain't afraid of my mom, are you, Clint?"

"Well, as a matter of fact, Tad," Clint said. "I am, kind of."

"Wow." The boy's eyes widened, and he turned

away from his aunt's horse to face Clint. "How come?"

"Because moms are very strong people," Clint answered. "Especially when it comes to their children."

"Really?"

"Really."

The boy thought a moment, then looked at Clint and said, "Well, my mom's sorta sickly. She ain't really that strong."

Clint crouched down in front of the boy and held his arms.

"Tad, I'm not talking about being physically strong, I'm talking about being strong in a way that only moms can be. I'm talking about being strong inside, and knowing what's best for their children, and not letting anything happen to them."

"Oh," Tad said, "that kind of strong."

"Yes," Clint said, "that kind."

"Well," Tad said, looking down, "I guess in that way she is kinda strong, huh?"

"I think she is," Clint said. "Come on, let's finish with these horses. I think I could use a nice cup of your mom's coffee."

Out in front of the house, as Clint and Tad led the horses away, Rachel Holt stepped up onto the porch and looked at her brother. For a moment she thought he didn't notice her, but he did. It's just that he was staring straight out, looking at . . . what? she wondered. Or was he . . . waiting?

"Where's Libby?"

"Inside," Ned said. He didn't offer any hint as to what his wife might be doing.

"What are you doing sitting out here with that rifle, Ned?"

He looked up at her for the first time.

"I'm waiting, Rachel."

"For what, Ned?"

He hesitated a moment, then said, "Well, for you and Clint to come back, for one thing. Clint and I have to go out after that wolf. Remember?"

"I remember, Ned."

"So I guess that means that I'm waiting for that wolf too."

"I see."

"And I'm waiting for Libby to get dinner ready," he said. "I guess I'm just waiting for a lot of things."

"I see," Rachel said again.

Ned nodded and looked away from her, staring straight out ahead of him again.

"Ned?"

"Yeah?"

"Is there anything you'd like to tell me?"

Ned thought a moment, then said, "No, not that I can think of."

"Nothing at all?"

He looked at her again.

"What did you have in mind, Sis?"

For a moment she was tempted to tell him all about their visit to the Gypsies, but she had agreed to let Clint talk to him about that.

"Oh, nothing," she said, moving closer and touching her brother's shoulder affectionately. "We just haven't talked in a long time."

"We're talking now." He either had no idea what she meant, or was pretending he didn't. "Ain't we?"

"Yes, Ned," she said, patting his shoulder now, "yes, I suppose we are."

She patted his shoulder once more, then went inside to see what her sister-in-law was doing.

# TWENTY-SIX

When Clint came back around to the front with Tad, he saw Ned still sitting on the porch.

"Hey, Tad," he said, "why don't you go inside? I want to talk to your dad for a while."

"Forget it," Tad said, mistaking Clint's intention. "I already tried. He's on my mom's side."

Clint laughed and said, "Well, I'll just give it a try. How about that?"

"Okay," Tad said. "Good luck."

"Thanks."

The boy went into the house while Clint went over and sat in the chair next to Ned's.

"Waiting for the wolf?" Clint asked.

"Waitin' on you is more like it," Ned said. "Now that you're back, maybe we can get started."

"Tell me about the wolf, Ned."

"Huh?" Ned turned his head and looked at Clint. "What do I know about the wolf? I ain't never even seen him."

"Oh, I think you have," Clint said. "Think about it, Ned. You've seen him, haven't you?"

Ned turned away, staring straight out again, only he wasn't looking out there. He was looking inside his head.

"Well," he said, licking his lips, "to tell you the truth, I have seen it . . . but you'll laugh . . ."

"No, Ned," Clint said, "I won't laugh. Where have you seen it?"

Ned looked at Clint and said, "I've seen it . . . in my dreams."

Clint stared at the man long enough to satisfy himself that he was telling the truth—or that he at least believed what he was saying.

"How many times, Ned?"

"How many times what?"

"How many times have you dreamed about the wolf?" Clint asked.

Ned frowned, then said, "A lot. At least . . . six or seven times."

"And is it the same animal each time?"

Ned thought a moment, then nodded and said, "Yeah . . . yeah, it is."

"And how many spells have you had?"

Ned thought for a moment, then stared at Clint wide-eyed.

"About the same amount."

"Now see if you can remember this, Ned." Clint's excitement was mounting, but he wasn't sure why. He didn't believe this stuff, after all.

"What?"

"Did you have your spells on the same nights you had the dream?"

"I can't remember. . . ."

"Try, Ned," Clint said. "Just think about it for a minute."

Ned nodded, and his eyes sort of went out of focus as he stared at something only he could see. After a few moments he turned his head and looked at Clint again.

"I can't be sure it was *every* time," he said very slowly, "but I can remember three—no, four times when I had a spell the same night I had the dream."

"Three or four," Clint said. "It was probably every time."

"But . . . how could that be?" Ned asked.

Clint wondered again about hypnosis, but shook his head to dispel any thoughts of that.

"Ned, how many times have you been to see Martika?" Clint asked.

"Martika?" Ned asked. "What has she got to do with this?"

"I think you should tell me that," Clint said. "She's the one who told you about the wolf, isn't she?"

"Well, yeah . . . her and her mother," Ned said. "It was the old lady who told me I had . . . the mark." He touched his face when he said it.

"Ned . . ." Clint said, and then he stopped. He knew he was going to ask the question, but he still felt silly asking it.

"What?"

"Ned . . . did you look into Martika's eyes?"

"Have you seen her, Clint?"

"I've seen her."

"Then you know," Ned said. "Sure, I looked into her eyes. Why?"

"Did anything happen when you did?"

"I wish it had," Ned said fervently. "But no, nothing happened. I wish, though. God, but she's beautiful, ain't she?"

"Yes," Clint said, "she's very beautiful. Ned, do you think Martika could have talked you into believing . . . well, before I ask you that, let's get our cards on the table, okay?"

"Okay."

"What do you think is happening to you?"

Ned stared at Clint for what seemed like a few minutes, then he shook his head and closed his eyes.

"I don't know what's happening to me," Ned said honestly. "But I can tell you one thing."

"What?"

Ned opened his eyes, and Clint could see the anguish in them.

"I'm scared."

"I guess you've got reason to be, Ned."

"I gotta kill that wolf, Clint. I don't know what's happening, but I do know I gotta kill that wolf."

"Ned," Clint said, "you don't think you turn into a wolf that walks like a man, do you?"

"God help me," Ned said, "I don't want to think it."

"But you do?"

Slowly Ned said, "I think it's . . . possible."

"It isn't, Ned," Clint said. "Let me tell you, it just isn't possible."

"Clint," Ned said, "what happens if we go out hunting for the wolf, and then you find out that . . . that *I'm* the wolf. What happens then?"

"That's not going to happen."

"But what if it does? You could get killed, Clint. I could kill you."

"Ned—"

"Or you could kill me."

"Ned—"

"Except that Martika said that a bullet won't kill the wolf that walks like a man," Ned went on. "She said that you need a—"

"Ned!" Clint yelled, loud enough to startle the man into silence.

"What?"

"In the morning we'll go out and find that wolf," Clint said. "I'll prove to you that a bullet will kill it—I'll prove to you that it's just a wolf."

"Just a wolf," Ned repeated.

"That's right," Clint said. He put his hand on Ned's shoulder and said, "Let's go inside."

# TWENTY-SEVEN

Later that night Clint was sitting on the porch with a cup of coffee. Tad was asleep, and Ned was in his bed. Libby and Rachel were inside cleaning up. When the door opened, he expected it to be Rachel, but was surprised to see that it was Ned's wife.

"Hello, Libby."

"Hello, Clint," she said. "Do you mind if I sit with you awhile?"

"No," he said, "have a seat."

She sat next to him and folded her arms, hugging herself.

"Are you and Ned going out in the morning after the wolf?"

"Yes."

"Do you think that if you kill it . . . Ned's spells will stop?"

"I don't know, Libby," Clint said. "I just thought we'd take things one step at a time."

She nodded.

"Libby, about Tad . . ."

"I'm sorry, Clint," she said, "but I don't want

you showing him how to fire your gun. I hate guns."

"Libby," he said, "if we kill this wolf and Ned's spells stop, it will be the result of a gun. You realize that, don't you?"

"That's—that's self-defense."

"As far as I'm concerned," he told her, "that's what all guns are for, self-defense."

She looked at him and said, "But . . . your reputation . . ."

"Libby, I never killed a man in cold blood," Clint said. "In fact, I never killed a man except to save my life . . . or the life of a friend."

She stared at him for a moment, then her face seemed to relax. She even smiled.

"I should have known that," she said. "You're a decent man, Clint. That's why you're here, trying to help us. That's why Rachel likes you . . . and Tad. . . ."

"Well . . . I hope you like me too, Libby."

"I do, Clint," she said, "I truly do, but I still don't want you to show Tad how to shoot your gun."

"Well, that's entirely up to you, Libby," Clint said. "Tad's your son. I'll abide by your wishes."

"Thank you, Clint," she said. "I knew you'd understand."

She stood up to go inside, but stopped at the door and looked at him.

"You will look out for Ned tomorrow, won't you?" she asked.

"Of course I will," Clint said. "Don't worry. This will all turn out all right."

"I hope so," she said. "I hope to God it will, for I know I will not survive without my husband. Good night, Clint."

"Good night, Libby."

The next time the door opened, about fifteen minutes later, it was Rachel. She had a fresh cup of coffee for Clint, who had an empty cup between his feet on the porch floor.

"Thanks," he said, accepting it from her.

She sat down next to him, pulling the shawl she was wearing tightly around her shoulders.

"I put some whiskey in it," she said. "I hope that's all right."

Clint sipped the hot coffee and felt the whiskey burn, both warming him.

"It's fine."

"What did you tell Libby?"

"That everything will be all right."

"And will it?"

"I don't know, Rachel."

"I want to come with you tomorrow, Clint," she said. "With you and Ned."

"No."

"Why not?"

"Can you shoot?"

"Well, no. . . ."

"Of course you can't," he said. "You're a teacher. I'd be a fool to take you with me when I'm hunting a wolf, Rachel."

"I won't get killed," she said sternly. "I can take care of myself."

"I'm not worried about you getting killed,"

Clint said, "I'm worried about me getting killed."

"What?"

"I'll be so concerned with your safety that I might get careless with my own," he explained. "I wouldn't want that to happen, Rachel, and neither would you."

"Well, what am I supposed to do while you and my brother are out hunting?"

"Stay here with your family."

She rubbed her upper arms and said, "They're not my family, they're his."

"Don't you consider his family to be yours as well?" Clint asked.

"No . . . well, yes . . . I mean . . . oh, I don't know," she said. "I'm thirty-four years old, Clint. I should have a family of my own by now. A husband, and children. . . ."

"Why don't you?" he asked. "You're beautiful, and intelligent; any man would be happy to have you as his wife."

"Would you?"

He did not let himself be flustered by the question.

"If I was the marrying kind, yes, Rachel," he said with a smile.

"But you're not, right?"

"No, I'm not."

"Why not?"

"Too old, too set in my ways, I guess. . . ."

"Not so old," she said. "Believe me, I know."

"Why, thank you, ma'am."

Suddenly she blushed.

"I wish we were back in your hotel," she said.
"So do I."

"I think we could get away with a kiss, don't you?" she asked.

He leaned over and kissed her softly on the mouth.

"I sure do."

He kissed her again, hungrily this time, both of their mouths opening, and then she pulled away breathlessly.

"That's as far as I think we can go here," she said. "I'm going to bed. What about you?"

"Soon," he said, looking down at his cup. "I want to finish this coffee first."

"I'll see you in the morning," she said, standing up.

"We'll be getting an early start, Rachel."

"Don't worry," she said, "I'll be awake."

"Then I'll see you in the morning."

"Good night," she said, and went inside.

Clint sat and finished his whiskey-laced coffee, looking out at the blackness. The wolf was out there somewhere.

At least, he hoped it was.

From the darkness a pair of predatory eyes were watching Clint Adams. The lights of the house, its warmth, and the smell of the animals behind it had attracted attention. Clint was too far away to see the feral glow of the eyes that were watching him. The eyes narrowed, and a wet tongue came out to lick a cold muzzle. The eyes continued to watch until

Clint went back into the house and the lights went out.

With a low growl, the predator moved slowly toward the house.

# TWENTY-EIGHT

The wolf was an old one, its coat gray and
shaggy. Ned Holt watched as the animal moved
toward him. He was helpless, frozen in his
tracks, unable to move at all while the animal
came closer and closer. Finally, he could feel
the heat from the huge body and the animal's
hot breath on his face.

Ned was lying in the snow. In contrast to
the beast's hot breath on one cheek, the other
cheek was pressed into the snow, numb. In
fact, his whole body was numb, except for his
face.

The wolf sniffed at Ned's body, nudging it
with its muzzle. Ned knew that if he didn't
move, the animal would think he was dead
and would begin to feast on him. If he moved,
maybe he could frighten the creature away.
He concentrated, trying to move at least one
arm, but it was useless. He was paralyzed and
could only watch helplessly as the wolf's mouth
opened and saliva dripped. It dropped into the
snow right in front of Ned's eyes and turned

to steam. The wolf was so old it was missing some teeth, but there were enough there to do the job. Ned closed his eyes as he felt the beast's fetid breath engulf him. He knew in moments the sharp teeth would close on his throat, tearing the flesh and ending his life. . . .

Ned woke breathlessly. He sat up quickly and fought for one breath, his body covered with sweat. Suddenly he was able to take that first deep breath, and then another.

He looked down at Libby, lying next to him, still fast asleep. Why was it that she never woke up when he was having a nightmare? How could she lie next to him and be completely unaware of the horror he was experiencing?

He swung his feet to the floor and sat with his elbows on his knees, his head in his hands. Suddenly, he felt as if something was in his head, as if something was calling to him.

He got up, walked to the window, and looked out. It was still dark, and snowing, but there was enough moonlight for him to see the shed where the horses were. From here the only horse he could make out was Clint Adams's big, black gelding, and that was because, for some reason, the horse was standing out in front of the shed, as if he was on guard.

There was a strip of moonlight on the snow that seemed to form a shining path from the house to the shed. In that path he was able to make out the tracks—wolf tracks.

It was happening again.

•  •  •

In the shed the horses began to shift and
snort. Duke felt the proximity of something
dangerous. The massive animal moved about
in the shed until he was able to look outside.
Not only could he feel that danger was near,
but he could smell it as well.

Since there was no corral and no way to lock
the shed, the other horses were all tied off. Duke
was the only one who was free. He walked outside and stood in the snow in front of the shed.
He was standing there only a minute when he
saw the wolf. Every massive muscle in his body
tensed as he waited for the wolf to attack.

The predator saw the black gelding in front
of the shed and stopped in his tracks. The wolf
knew there was food behind the black horse,
but in order to get to it he was going to have to
get past the big horse. That would mean a noisy
battle that he might or might not win. The old
lobo was not willing to risk it. He turned and
instead walked toward the house.

# TWENTY-NINE

In the morning when Libby Holt awoke without her husband beside her, she assumed that he had already risen to go hunting with Clint Adams. When she came out of their bedroom and did not see either man, and saw that Ned's rifle was gone, and realized that it was still early, she panicked and began pounding on the door to Tad's room, where Clint was sleeping.

Clint came to the door quickly.

"Libby? What is it?"

"He's gone, Clint," she said. "Ned's gone."

"What?"

Rachel, who slept on a pallet in the living room, awoke and asked, "What's going on?"

"I'll get dressed," Clint told Libby. Turning to Rachel, he said, "Ned's gone."

"Jesus . . ." Rachel said.

While Clint was getting dressed, Tad woke up, and Clint told him what was happening. The boy got up and dressed quickly. Clint strapped on his gun.

"Tad," Clint said, "check the horses, see if your dad's is still there."

"Yes, sir."

They came out of the room at the same time. Rachel was sitting at the kitchen table with her arm around Libby, consoling her.

Clint and Tad went to the front door. The Gunsmith was hoping that Ned was simply sitting on the porch and Libby hadn't looked there, but that wasn't the case. Tad rushed around the house, and Clint looked straight out from the house. There were fresh tracks in the snow leading away from the house, toward the thick woods a few hundred yards away.

Tad came back around the house, running and breathing hard.

"Clint, I think you better come. . . ."

Clint looked at the boy, then said, "Let's go."

He followed the boy around to the back and saw Duke standing outside the shed instead of inside. His black coat was wet and glistening from the snow. How long had he been standing there?

"What's he doing outside?" Tad asked.

"Let's look around and find out."

They walked toward the back of the house until Clint saw the tracks.

"There," he said, pointing to the wolf tracks in the snow, "that's why Duke is out of the shed."

"The wolf?" Tad asked, his eyes widening. "It came this close to the house?"

"It was after the horses, for food, but it couldn't get past Duke."

"You mean he protected the other horses?" Tad asked in amazement.

"That's right, Tad," Clint said. "Is your father's horse still in the shed?"

"Yes."

"Then he's on foot," Clint said.

"What will you do?"

"I'll have to go after him," Clint said. "I'll saddle Duke and you saddle your dad's horse for me. I'll take it with me."

"All right."

Quickly they saddled both horses and then walked them around to the front of the house. Both women had come out on the porch.

"What's happening?" Rachel asked.

"I'll let Tad tell you," Clint said. "Tad, go inside and get my rifle."

"Are you leaving now?" Rachel asked.

"I've got to go after Ned."

Libby looked at Ned's horse and said, "He's on foot, isn't he?"

"Yes."

"He'll be killed this time," she said, shaking her head. "I know it."

"Be quiet, Libby," Rachel said sternly. "Go inside and get Clint some food."

Libby did not argue. She went into the house.

"Clint—"

"The wolf was here last night, Rachel," Clint said, now that Libby was gone. "It tried to get the horses."

"You think Ned went after it?"

"Ned's tracks lead straight out," Clint said, "as do the wolf's. Apparently he didn't want to take the time to saddle his horse."

"You've got to catch up to him."

"I know."

Tad came out with Clint's rifle and a burlap sack of food.

"Momma packed this," he said, handing it to Clint.

"Thanks."

Clint took the sack and tied it to his saddle.

"Can I come, Clint?" the boy asked. "I want to help my dad."

"Tad," Clint said, "I need you here, to take care of your mother and your aunt. Can you do that?"

The boy puffed out his chest and said, "Yes, sir. You can count on me."

Clint looked at Rachel and asked, "Is there a weapon in the house?"

"Yes," Rachel said, "a rifle."

"Can you use it?"

Rachel shook her head helplessly and started to say, "I suppose . . ."

"I can shoot it," Tad said. "I'm a good shot."

"Tad—" Rachel said.

"No," Clint said, "he's right, Rachel. Of the three of you, he's the one who can shoot. Tad, keep that rifle handy, all right? With me and Duke gone, that wolf might come back for the horses."

"Yes, sir," the boy said, wide-eyed again.

"If it comes back," Clint said, "don't leave the house. Do you understand? Don't let your aunt or your mother leave the house. If you want to take a shot at it, do it from a window. Do you understand me, Tad?"

"Yes, sir, I do."

"Rachel?"

"We understand, Clint," Rachel said, putting her hands on the boy's shoulders. "You be careful. Take care of yourself, and my brother. Do you hear me?"

"I hear you, Rachel," Clint said. "We'll be back soon—both of us."

# THIRTY

Fortunately, the tracks were not hard to follow. Clint was used to tracking men, who usually left some sign behind them that was fairly simple to pick up—broken branches, overturned rocks on the ground, cold camp fires. Most of the hunting of animals Clint had done had been during the days when he was hunting buffalo with Bat Masterson and Wyatt Earp—and that was *many* years ago.

Tracking a wolf was not something Clint felt he was good at. A man like Vin Hacker, now he could probably track a wolf through water. He knew what to look for.

What was making it easy to track this wolf was that Clint was also tracking Ned Holt—and both the animal and the man were leaving a trail in the snow that was easy to see. The only thing Clint couldn't figure was who was following who. This was because the tracks never overlapped. He didn't find a wolf print inside a man's shoe print, which would have meant that the man's print was left first, nor did he find any trampled wolf tracks. All he knew was that man and wolf were moving in the same direction. He assumed that Ned had left the house to track the wolf, but at some point that could have changed. The wolf could have doubled back and turned the man into the prey. Clint had no way of knowing this, unless some of the tracks finally started to cross.

Clint had been tracking for half the day, moving slowly because he was dragging Ned's horse behind him, when he finally caught a break. He found another set of wolf tracks which came from his right and then fell in behind the established wolf and man tracks. This could have meant that a second wolf had joined the fun, but he didn't think so. He got down and examined both sets of wolf tracks closely, until he became convinced that they had been made by the same animal. This meant that the wolf *had* doubled back on Ned, and now the man was being tracked by the wolf.

This might have been a break for Clint, because he knew what was happening now, but it certainly was no kind of break for Ned.

Ned Holt was tired. He was standing in the middle of the woods, looking toward the mountains. At least this time he knew how he had come to be there. He remembered perfectly seeing the wolf behind his house, remembered dressing quickly, leaving his room, grabbing his rifle, and running out of his house. By that time the wolf was gone, probably scared off by the prospect of tangling with Clint Adams's big, black gelding. There was a brave animal.

When he got outside and discovered that the wolf had run off, he found the beasts's tracks in the snow and began to track him on foot. He did not even want to take the time to saddle his horse, or wake up Clint Adams. He wanted that wolf so badly that he immediately took off after him on foot.

Which at the time had seemed like the right thing to do.

But on second thought . . .

Ned stared down at the wolf's tracks in the snow. Abruptly, they turned and went off to his right. He'd tracked enough game to know that the animal had doubled back on him.

The hunter had now become the hunted.

Suddenly, Ned Holt just wanted to lie down in the snow and sleep . . . just give up.

# THIRTY-ONE

Clint figured the wolf was now somewhere between him and Ned. That meant that he'd have to come upon the wolf first—at least, that was what he thought. That was why he was surprised when he saw the man lying in the snow.

At first he thought the man was dead, but there was no blood in the snow. He left the two horses where they were and approached the body. As he got closer, he saw that it was Ned Holt, still breathing.

What would happen when he woke up? Clint wondered. Would he remember anything that had happened? Was this another one of his spells?

He approached the fallen man and went down on one knee beside him. It was almost like reliving the first time he'd come upon the man. He touched Ned's shoulder and turned him over. He was shocked to find Ned staring at him as he rolled onto his back. Clint had seen many men die with their eyes open in a perpetual stare, and for a moment he thought this might be the case with Ned, but then the man blinked.

"Ned?"

"Clint?"

"Come on," Clint said. "Sit up. Are you hurt?"

"No," Ned said, as Clint hauled him into a seated position, "I don't seem to be."

"Do you know who I am?" Clint asked, even though the man had already called him by name.

"Yes, I do."

"Do you know who you are?"

"Of course I do."

"Okay," Clint said, "now here's the big question. Do you know how you got here?"

Ned frowned, thinking for a moment, then nodded and said, almost in awe, "Y-yes, I do . . . I actually know what happened."

"Then tell me."

Ned told Clint about his dream, and about waking up, looking out the window, and seeing the wolf.

"He couldn't get to the horses because of your horse," Ned said. "That's quite an animal you've got there."

"I know," Clint said. "After that you followed him all this way on foot?"

"Yes," Ned said, "right to here, when he doubled back on me."

"I saw that," Clint said, "and I don't get it. If he doubled back on you and got on your trail, that means he was between you and me, and yet I reached you before he did."

"How did that happen?" Ned asked.

"There's only one way I can think of."

"What's that?"

"That's the way he wanted it," Clint said. He looked around and said, "He could be out there somewhere right now, watching us."

"What do we do?" Ned asked.

"I brought your horse," Clint said. "Let's get mounted up and find someplace to camp for the night. We can decide what to do then."

"All right."

"Can you stand?"

"Yes."

Clint helped him to his feet, but Ned didn't need any help walking.

"I don't understand this," Ned said. "I had the dream and followed the wolf, but I didn't have one of my spells. Why?"

"We'll talk about that too, after we've camped," Clint said. "Right now let's get out of here. If this is where he wants us, then we definitely don't want to be here."

After they mounted up, they rode for about half an hour before finding a clearing where they could camp. Clint took care of the horses while Ned saw to building a fire. The man was suffering none of the effects of the previous spells, of which Clint had only seen one. They were both wondering as they saw to their chores why this time had been different from the others.

Once the fire was going, they made coffee and

cooked some vegetables that Libby had put into the sack for them.

"Tell me about the dream," Clint said, and Ned related it in all its horror.

"Was that like the other dreams?"

"Sort of."

"How was it different?"

"Well, in the other dreams I was able to move," Ned said. "In the early ones the wolf was tracking me, and I was running." The dreams were coming back to him now. "In the later ones I was tracking it. This is the first time I've ever been totally helpless."

It was interesting to Clint, but he was not equipped to be able to tell what it all meant—if it meant anything at all.

"Did you see the wolf at all last night after you left the house?"

"No," Ned said, "I just followed its tracks."

Clint rubbed his jaw.

"I still can't figure what happened to it after it doubled back and got between you and me," Clint said.

"Maybe it heard you coming and ran off," Ned offered.

"Maybe," Clint said, "but this animal doesn't strike me as the timid type."

"It wouldn't go up against your Duke last night," Ned reminded him.

"That just makes it smart," Clint said. "Duke's hooves would have caved in its skull."

"Are you sure that the second set of tracks

you saw were the same as the first?"

"They looked identical to me," Clint said, "but I'm not a wolfer—which reminds me."

He told Ned about the wolfer, Vin Hacker, being in town.

"The only reason Vin would be here is either for the bounty, or because he was hired," Clint said, then added, "and maybe both."

"Then he might be out here right now hunting the wolf?" Ned asked.

"It's possible."

"Then maybe the wolf heard him."

"Maybe."

"What do we do now?"

"We'll take turns on watch and get an early start in the morning," Clint said. "We're going to have to backtrack and see if we can't pick up his trail again."

"This is a smart animal, Clint," Ned said. "I can feel it. Last night when I woke up I felt like someone was inside my head."

Clint dismissed that thought almost as soon as Ned said it. He couldn't afford to allow himself to start believing things like that.

It was bad enough they were dealing with an animal who was intelligent; he didn't want to start believing in one who was supernatural as well.

A pair of predatory eyes watched the two humans sitting at the fire. The animal knew instinctively that it could not attack, not when there were two together this way. Also, the fire was not something that it wanted to get too close to.

As the sky began to grow darker, the animal started to walk in circles around the camp, keeping its eyes on the two humans the whole time. There would come a time when both were not up and moving.

# THIRTY-TWO

Clint took the first watch in order to give immediate rest to Ned Holt. Also, he wanted to sit up and give some thought to everything that was going on.

Obviously they were dealing with a real wolf, not some figment of a Gypsy's imagination. Holt had seen the wolf, and Clint had seen the tracks. A real wolf could be killed by a real bullet. Luckily, Ned's rifle had been on the ground next to him and was still in working order. Between the two of them, one of them ought to be able to put a bullet in the wolf—either them, or Vin Hacker, or anyone else who was hunting for it.

Clint really didn't care who killed it as long as it was killed. For the sake of the Holt family, though, he hoped that either he or Ned would get it. They could put the thousand-dollar bounty to very good use.

There was also something that he and the others seemed to have forgotten, and that was the unfortunate dead man he'd found before he

ran across Ned. He'd neglected to ask the sheriff who the man was and hadn't talked to the
doctor about what exactly killed him. He was
curious now, but he knew his curiosity would
have to go unsatisfied for a while longer.

Clint poured himself another cup of coffee,
being careful not to look into the fire. In fact,
he tossed some more wood onto the fire. If the
wolf was out in the darkness looking at them,
it was going to be sure to stay away from the
flames—especially if the animal was as smart
as it seemed to be. Next to man, fire was probably its worst enemy. With Clint sitting at the
camp fire, it would have had to deal with its
two worst enemies at one time, which seemed
unlikely.

He drank his coffee slowly and thought about
the Gypsies. Did they even believe the stories
they were telling about werewolves? He was
sure the old woman did, because she was
probably from the old country—wherever that
was—but what about the younger ones? Erik,
Martika, and even Erik's son, Nicholas? What
were they teaching him? And what about the
two men he hadn't met, Erik's father and
uncle?

In the long run, however, none of that mat-
tered. All they had to do now was make sure
that the wolf was killed and that Ned stopped
thinking that he was a wolf that walked on
two feet.

Jesus, Clint thought, the things people could
be made to believe.

• • •

In another part of the wood, Vin Hacker sat
at his fire and thought about his job. Getting
rid of the wolf would be the easiest part. He had
never failed to kill a wolf once he got on its trail.
The second part of the job, killing Ned Holt,
shouldn't be a problem either. The third part,
however, was Clint Adams. Hacker didn't kid
himself that he could beat Adams in a gunfight,
but then they weren't in that arena. They were
out here in the woods, on a hunt, and that put
Clint Adams in Vin Hacker's environment.

Out here Hacker was sure that Clint Adams
was no match for him, although he was in no
way underestimating the man. He had seen
Clint Adams in action. But once he killed
Adams and let the word get out, his reputation
as a hunter and his fame would extend far and
wide—and with that the opportunities to make
more money than he ever had before. Once he
became the man who killed the Gunsmith, he'd
be able to name his own price for jobs.

He looked over at Crow Woman, the Indian
girl who cooked his meals and made his clothes.
He had traded for her with some mountain men
who had wanted some of his wolf hides. She'd
been with him four months, and he was happy
with her performance. She kept him well fed,
his clothes were well made, and she shared his
bedroll. She wasn't real big, but she was warm
and made for a comfortable night each night.
It was a hell of a lot better than sleeping alone.
He still longed for white women when he got

to town, but when he was on the hunt, Crow Woman took care of his every need.

They were finished eating and she was cleaning up, but Hacker suddenly had the urge for sex.

"Come here," he said to her.

She looked at him across the fire. She was in her early twenties, and although she was small, she was solidly built. He liked that, as well as her long black hair and the fact that she had good teeth.

"I must finish cleaning—" she started to say, but he interrupted her.

"I said come here, Crow Woman. I want a poke . . . now!"

Crow Woman heaved a great sigh, got up, and walked around to his side of the fire. She had a name, but he had been calling her Crow Woman for months and she no longer thought of herself any other way.

She sat next to him, and he roughly thrust his hand inside her buckskin top. He took one of her firm breasts in his hands and squeezed it. Then Hacker pinched her nipple and pressed his mouth against her neck. She tried to ignore the smell of him and his wet saliva dripping down her neck while she moaned the way she knew he liked her to.

She'd been waiting months for a chance to slip a knife between his ribs, and she'd wait as long as it took for the perfect moment to come along. She didn't want to try to kill him and fail, because then he'd break her neck for sure.

He pulled her top off so that she was naked to her waist and then pushed her down onto her back on his blanket. He began sucking and biting her nipples, and his saliva turned cold on her skin as soon as the chilled air hit it. He used one hand to work his own britches down until his erection was exposed, stiff and pulsing. Roughly, he pulled her buckskin trousers down around her ankles, then mounted her. She was dry, not wet the way a woman was supposed to be when her man entered her, but then she didn't think of him as her man. She thought of him as her captor. As he snorted and groaned, pounding into her, she gazed at the sky, at the stars, and tried to will herself away from her body until he was finished. . . .

Erik St. Jermaine looked across the fire at his sister, Martika. They were still waiting for their father and uncle to return from their hunt, but it was getting late. They had been out for days and should have been back long ago. Nicholas, Erik's son, was asleep underneath their wagon, while their mother was asleep in hers.

"We cannot wait any longer," Erik said finally. He dumped the remnants of his coffee into the fire, causing the flames to flare.

"What are you going to do?" Martika asked.

"I will have to go and look for them," Erik said, "and for the wolf. I will take Nicholas with me."

"I will come."

"No."

"You forget, Brother," Martika said, "I have a power you do not. The wolf will not kill me."

He glared at her across the fire, and she saw the flickering flames reflected in his eyes. He was her older brother and he loved her, but sometimes he resented the special power that she had. He was the man and she was the woman, and he was supposed to protect her. When she reminded him that she didn't need his protection, he did not like it at all.

But in this instance he knew that she was right.

"All right," he said, "you will come. I will leave Nicholas here with Momma."

"When we find the wolf," she said, "I will handle him, Erik. If I can talk to him, perhaps he will not have to be killed."

"He is out of control, Martika," Erik said, shaking his head. "He has killed a man. He has the taste again. He will not be easy to control."

"I know," she said, "but we must try . . . we must. . . ."

# THIRTY-THREE

Clint woke on his own in the morning, before Ned had a chance to wake him. He was half afraid that he would wake up and find Ned gone, but the man was there, sitting at the fire, keeping watch.

When Clint came up next to Ned, he startled the man, who looked up at him.

"I was just gonna wake you."

"It's all right," Clint said. "Is that coffee fresh?"

"I just made it."

Clint hunkered down next to Ned and poured himself a cup of coffee.

"What about breakfast?" Ned asked.

"This is breakfast."

"In that case," Ned said, "I better have me another cup."

After "breakfast" they broke camp. Ned doused the fire, and Clint saddled the horses. Clint would always handle the horses because it was doubtful that Ned could ever have handled Duke.

Once the fire was good and dead and they had packed up, they mounted up and rode back the way they had come. Clint reasoned that since it hadn't rained or snowed during the night, whatever trail there had been the day before should still be there.

They rode back first to the point where Clint had found Ned yesterday. Ned remained mounted while Clint stepped down to examine the ground.

"Are you good at this?" Ned asked.

"Good at what?"

"Tracking?"

Clint stared at the ground a few more moments before looking up at him.

"I've tracked men before," Clint said, "but I'm no expert at hunting animals. Let's just hope that what I do know will do the trick." Pointing, he said, "This is where he doubled back. You saw that yesterday."

"Yes, I did."

"We'll follow this trail and see where it leads," Clint said, remounting Duke.

"Keep that rifle ready," he added. "If this wolf is as smart as everyone says, than he's going to be unpredictable as well."

"I know that," Ned said. "He's already different from any wolf I've ever run across."

"Have you run across many?"

"Not that many," Ned said. "This is sure the first one that ever got into my dreams."

• • •

Vin Hacker broke camp and started his hunt in earnest. He studied the ground for tracks, but that didn't mean his eyes were always cast downward. Hacker was a trained tracker, and he knew that sign was not always found on the ground.

Crow Woman walked behind him as he rode. She was limping slightly because he had wanted sex again when they woke up that morning. He had been rough with her the night before, and even rougher today, and she was feeling the effects of his abuse.

"Come on, come on," he shouted at her, "keep up or I'll leave you behind."

He had said that to her before. Once she decided to test him. She lagged behind, and instead of leaving her he had come back and beaten her for not keeping up. After that she kept up, no matter how hard it was.

But both Hacker and Crow Woman knew that he kept her around for a different reason . . .

Once, about a week after he had traded her with the mountain men, they had been camped. It was in the mountains, near the Powder River. She was cooking for him, sitting on the other side of the fire, when she suddenly froze.

Hacker was eating, finishing his first plate of food, and when he held his plate out for her to refill, he saw that she was sitting stock-still.

"Hey!" he snapped. "I want more."

She didn't move.

"What the hell is the matter with you?" he demanded loudly.

"Wolf," she said softly.

He didn't hear her.

"What?"

Slowly she focused her eyes on him and said, still very quietly, "Wolf."

He stared at her, then slowly put his plate down between his legs. He reached beside him for his Sharps. It was a buffalo gun, and in fact he had used it for many years to hunt buffalo, until he started hunting wolf. He owned a Winchester, but he usually made his killing shot with the Sharps.

"Where?"

He didn't ask her how she knew—not then, anway.

She closed her eyes and breathed in, then opened them and pointed to her left—west.

"There."

"How close?"

"Very close."

She remained seated at the fire while he stood up, Sharps in his hands.

"Coming closer . . ." she said.

"Jesus," he said, "it's coming right up to the camp?"

"I do not know," she said, "I only know that it is coming closer. . . ."

Hacker moved to the edge of the camp very slowly, as if to wait there for the arrival of the animal. He had sharp eyes and detected a movement in the brush—but he knew he wouldn't have detected it without the woman. He raised the Sharps, and before the approaching wolf even knew what had happened a .50 caliber bullet exploded its heart.

Ignoring the dead animal—he *knew* it was dead, didn't even have to check—he walked back to the fire and the Indian woman and stared down at her.

"You can smell a wolf?"

She looked up at him and nodded.

That was the reason she was still with him. Not her cooking, or cleaning, or the sex, but the fact that she could usually—not always, but usually—smell a wolf if it was near.

She thought about *not* telling him if one was near on the off chance that it might kill him, but if that happened and it didn't kill him, he'd probably beat her.

So when she smelled a wolf she told him—and right now she smelled one. . . .

Erik and Martika slowed their horses to a walk.

"He's near," she said. "I feel him."

"How near?"

She closed her eyes for a moment, then opened them and shook her head.

"I don't know."

Erik stood up in his stirrups and looked around. All he could see was brush and trees. He closed his eyes and concentrated, but he couldn't feel or sense anything. Martika had always been the sensitive one. Their mother said that even as a child Martika had had the gift, the sight.

He settled back into his saddle and looked at his beautiful sister. Perhaps the only woman he had ever seen who rivaled her beauty was Rachel Holt.

"Let's keep riding," he said.

# THIRTY-FOUR

They stopped at midday, not to camp but to rest the horses—or more specifically, to rest Ned's horse. The animal was old and could not keep up with Duke.

They had followed the wolf's trail to the point where he had started to walk over his own tracks, and then they found something that Clint had missed yesterday. They found a point at which the wolf had veered off for some reason. It had given up its position behind Ned, possibly because it had heard Clint coming up behind it.

Or maybe it was just toying with them.

"What do we do now?" Ned asked.

"We follow the trail."

"Even if it might lead us into a trap?"

Clint shook his head.

"I don't know if I can accept that any animal is smart enough to lead us into a trap."

"Well, if there ever was one," Ned said, "it's this critter."

"Maybe . . ."

"What about food?" Ned asked. "The food
Libby gave you is almost gone."

"We've got water," Clint said, "and we ought
to be able to refill our canteens somewhere along
the way."

"That's it?" Ned asked. "We're going to live
on water?"

"Until we kill that wolf, yes."

"That's crazy."

"Ned," Clint said, looking at the man hard,
"this whole thing is crazy, isn't it?"

"Well . . . yeah . . ."

"And you want to get this wolf, don't you?"

"Oh, yeah, I do," Ned said, nodding, "more
than anything."

"More than eating?"

"Well . . ."

"Let's keep going," Clint said. "If this trail
keeps going straight, then we're going to end
up in the mountains. If that happens, we may
*have* to turn back."

"Maybe he stopped before he got to the mountains," Ned said. "After all, the easy game is
down here."

"Let's hope that's the way our wolf is thinking too," Clint said.

When Vin Hacker looked, he saw that Crow
Woman was almost twenty yards behind him.
He was about to shout at her to keep up when
he noticed that she was standing very still. He
turned his horse and rode back to her.

"Do you smell it?"

She looked up at him and nodded.

"So?"

"The odor is very strong," she said. "This is a very old wolf . . ." She stopped, looking puzzled.

"What is it?"

She shook her head.

"I do not know. This does not smell like any other wolf."

"What are you saying?" Hacker asked. "That this one is different?"

"Yes," she said, nodding, "it is different."

"Well," he said, "ain't never been a wolf so different that a fifty-caliber bullet couldn't stop him. Which way is it headed, Crow Woman?"

She hesitated, then pointed and said, "There."

"Toward the mountains?"

"Yes."

"Well, let's get goin' then," Hacker said. "There's liable to be some others after him too."

Coming from another direction, but also heading for the mountains, were Erik and Martika St. Jermaine.

"If he goes into the mountains, we will have a hard time finding him," Erik said.

"He won't go into the mountains," Martika said.

"Why not?"

She looked at her brother and said slowly, "He will not—at least, not so far up that we won't be able to follow him."

Erik looked around and said, "I wish at least we'd find Uncle."

Martika looked at Erik and said, "Maybe *he* is in the mountains."

Erik looked in the direction of the mountains, then looked at his sister again.

"Let's go right to the mountain, then," Erik said. "If he is headed that way, maybe we can be there waiting for him."

"Or we can find Uncle."

"Right now," Erik said, "I would settle for either one. Uncle could tell us what is going on."

Martika nodded, but she didn't really believe it. This time, she did not even think her uncle would be of much help. The burden of ending this once and for all was going to fall on her.

This is what her gift told her.

The object of the hunt stood very still, his wet muzzle in the air, sniffing. He could smell man, and more than one. He looked to the mountains, but he knew there was no game there. The mountains *would* offer refuge, but that wasn't what this very special animal was craving—and his craving, long dormant and now alive once again, was more than he could control.

It was more than he wanted to control.

It was a deep hunger, a primal thirst, that could only be satisfied by one kind of game.

The kind that was hunting him.

# THIRTY-FIVE

The first to reach the base of the mountains were the two Gypsies.

"We will dismount and wait here," Erik announced.

Martika did not reply. She dismounted and stood there, as if she were listening to something.

Exasperated with his little sister's gift, but knowing that they needed it to complete their mission, Erik said, "Yes, what?"

"Uncle," she said, looking up the slope. "He is up there."

"Up there?"

"Not far," she said. "There is this slope, and then the face of the mountain. He is at the top of the slope, probably in a cave. I cannot be sure."

"And the wolf?"

She closed her eyes for a minute. Then she shook her head and opened her eyes again.

"It is not with him."

"It is near?"

She closed her eyes once more, then shivered and hugged her arms, even though it had grown no colder than moments before.

"It is near," she said, nodding, "and it feels . . . different."

"Different how?"

"There is something I have never felt before," she said. "There is a hunger . . ."

"You have felt *that* before," he said testily.

"And something else."

He waited, and when she did not speak again, he said, "Well . . . what?"

"Erik," she said, staring at him, "there is a . . . a malevolence. . . ."

"You've never felt that before."

"No," she said. "It's very strong and . . . frightening."

He moved to her and put his hand on her shoulder. He felt her trembling.

"Sister," Erik said, "we must do this. . . ."

"I know," she said, covering his hand with hers, "I know. . . ."

Vin Hacker stopped his horse and held his hand out to Crow Woman to stop.

"What is it?" she asked.

"Now *I* smell something."

"What?"

He sniffed the air. She wondered how he could smell anything but himself.

"People."

"Men?" she asked.

"Men, and a woman—a sweet-smelling woman."

"What do we do?"

He turned in his saddle to look at her.

"We go on," he said. "Any woman who smells like that, I want to meet."

He turned and started his horse forward again. Crow Woman followed.

Clint and Ned rode on, following the tracks left in the snow by the wolf. The tracks were easy to follow because by now they were frozen in the snow. Even Ned had no trouble following them.

"This is too easy," Ned said.

Clint looked at him.

"Is that a complaint?"

"I'm just sayin'," Ned replied.

"Well," Clint said, "it's easy if these tracks actually do lead us to the wolf."

"And?"

"And not so easy if it's a trap."

Ned looked at Clint in surprise.

"I don't believe it."

"What?"

"Now you're talking like it's a trap?"

Clint thought a moment, startled, surprised at himself, and then said, "I guess I am."

"And what else are you believing?"

"Nothing."

"No?" Ned thought Clint had answered that question a little too quickly.

"No."

Ned studied Clint's profile for a moment, then shrugged. He wondered if it would take Clint as long to believe as it had taken him, then he realized that they didn't have that much time.

# THIRTY-SIX

Erik and Martika left their horses at the base of the slope and started walking up. The animals were skittish, so it was obvious to the siblings that the wolf was somewhere in the area. Erik looked back down the slope, but Martika tugged at his sleeve.

"There is nothing we can do for them but what we have done," she said.

What they had done for the horses was to leave them untethered, so that if—and when—the wolf arrived, they would have a chance to escape.

"Yes, you're right."

They ascended the slope, with not a gun between them, to find their uncle, and their father, and the horror that had been haunting them for years.

Perhaps here, at the base of this mountain, it might all come to an end.

Clint and Ned reached the clearing at the base of the mountain shortly after the Gypsies

and saw their horses milling about nervously.
About a hundred yards back, Ned's horse had
also gotten nervous. Duke was exhibiting no
outward signs of anxiety, but Clint had been
riding the big gelding a long time, and he could
feel the tension beneath him.

The wolf was near.

"Whose horses . . ." Ned started to ask, but
Clint had known the answer as soon as he saw
them.

"I saw those horses at the Gypsy camp," he
said.

"The Gypsies?" Ned said. "What the hell are
they doing here?"

"I had a feeling they knew more than they
were saying," Clint replied. "I guess maybe
we're about to find out what that is."

They rode up to the two horses and saw that
they were not tied.

"Why wouldn't they tie them?" Ned asked.
"Or ground the reins?"

"They wanted to give them a fighting chance
if the wolf showed up," Clint said. "We'll have
to do the same."

"What?"

"Leave the horses and go up the slope."

"Why?"

Clint pointed to the tracks in the snow.

"The Gypsies went up the slope."

"Yeah, but did the wolf?"

Clint fixed Ned with a stare. "I don't know if
you noticed or not, but the wolf tracks ended as
we entered this clearing."

Ned looked around quickly and saw that Clint was right. The tracks had ended.

"Well then, he didn't go up the slope, did he?" Ned reasoned.

"Where *did* he go then, Ned?" Clint asked. "There are no other tracks."

"You mean the tracks just . . . ended?"

"No," Clint said uncomfortably, "they didn't just end."

"Then what did happen?"

"The wolf tracks ended," Clint said, "and the tracks of a man began."

"You mean—"

"I mean just what I said and no more," Clint said quickly.

"Clint," Ned said, "don't you see what this means?"

"No," Clint said irritably, "I don't."

"The legend is true. . . ."

"Come on, Ned."

"There is a wolf that walks like a man . . ."

"Ned."

"And it ain't me!" Ned finished.

"Ned!"

"Well, I was with you all the time," Ned said. "If these wolf tracks turned into a man's tracks, that means it couldn't be me."

"Ned," Clint said, "I'm glad you realize that you're not a wolf who walks like a man, but now you've got to realize that there is no such thing at all."

"Well then, how do you explain those tracks?" Ned demanded.

Clint hesitated, then said, "There has to be a logical explanation for it, and I'll bet the Gypsies know what it is."

"So we're gonna follow them on up this slope?" Ned asked.

"That's right," Clint said.

Ned looked up the slope, then back at Clint. "What if the wolf's up there?"

"Well, that would be good, wouldn't it?" Clint asked. "I mean, we are hunting it, aren't we?"

"Oh, yeah," Ned said, "that's right, we are."

"Dismount," Clint said, "and take only your rifle. Leave your horse loose so he has a chance to get away if . . . if something happens."

Clint checked his rifle, then removed his Colt from his holster and checked that as well. He wanted to make sure both weapons were in proper working order. While doing that he was aware that Ned was mumbling something.

"Sure," Ned mumbled, dismounting, "give the *horse* a chance to get away . . ."

"What did you say?"

"Nothing," Ned said, taking his rifle in hand, "nothing at all."

They approached the slope and Clint asked, "What do you know about these mountains, Ned?"

"Not much," Ned replied. "There are some caves up there at the base, but that's as far as I've ever gone."

"What were you doing up there?"

Ned looked down at his feet, then looked at

Clint and said, "After one of my spells I woke up in one of the caves."

"Ned, could you find that cave again?"

"I guess so," he said. "But why?"

"Just a hunch," Clint said, "just a weird hunch."

They started up the slope.

It was only minutes later when Vin Hacker and Crow Woman came into the clearing. Hacker immediately recognized Clint Adams's horse.

"Many people here," Crow Woman said.

"Yeah," Hacker said, "it looks like. . . . But is the wolf here?"

"He is here," she said. "Somewhere."

Hacker nodded and rubbed his bearded jaw. If Clint Adams was here, that probably meant that the other fella, Ned Holt, was here also. There were four horses, though. Who did the other two belong to? Well, that didn't really matter. If they were going to get between him and his money—both his pay for the job and the bounty on the wolf—he'd take care of them the same way he did Adams and Holt—and the wolf.

"We're goin' up that slope," he said to Crow Woman. "You carry my Winchester and have it ready for me when I ask for it. Understand?"

She took the rifle from him and nodded slowly, thinking at the same time. If he wanted the Winchester it meant that he was going to kill some men. He held onto the Sharps, which he would use on the wolf.

When he came up against other men he was going to need the rifle, and he would expect her to give it to him. Crow Woman was sensing that this might be her chance to get away from Vin Hacker. She would only have to wait for her chance, and time it just right.

Hacker dismounted and left everything on his saddle, taking only his Sharps.

"Follow me up," he told her, "and stay close. We're gettin' to it now."

She agreed. They *were* getting to it.

## THIRTY-SEVEN

Inside the cave a man sat before a small fire, waiting. He had been waiting for days, living off of roots and whatever berries he could find and water from a nearby stream. When he heard the sound of feet scraping on the ground outside the cave, he looked up in time to see Erik and Martika enter.

"Uncle," Erik said.

"Erik," Uncle Elias St. Jermaine said. "Martika. What are you doing here?"

"Looking for you," Erik said.

"And Poppa," Martika said. "Where is he, Uncle?"

"Gone," Elias said.

He looked drawn and older than his sixty-one years. There were dark patches under his bloodshot eyes, and he looked even thinner than usual. His clothes, once brightly colored, were now covered with dirt and torn.

"When did you see him last?" Erik asked.

"Two days."

"And . . . the wolf?" Martika asked.

"I saw the wolf once," Elias said. "Two days ago."

"Did you notice anything about it?" Erik asked.

"Yes," Elias said, nodding sadly. He held his hand up in front of his face and said, "His muzzle was covered with . . . with blood."

"Damn," Erik said.

"We knew that, Erik," Martika said.

"He killed . . . a man, then?" Elias asked.

"Yes," Erik said.

The old man shook his head.

"Uncle," Erik said, "it's time for you to leave. Go back to the camp and wait."

"I cannot," Elias said. "He is my brother. I must wait. I must help him."

"He is beyond your help now, Uncle," Erik said. "We must leave it to Martika."

Their uncle looked at them with haunted eyes and said again, "He is my brother."

The statement hung in the air between them for a moment, and Erik and Martika took the opportunity to look around.

"Tell us about this cave," Erik said. "Why are you here?"

"This is where he will come."

"Are there other ways in and out?"

"Many," Elias said. "There are tunnels everywhere—some not large enough for a man."

The inference was clear. There were tunnels in this cave that only the wolf would be able to use.

Martika approached her uncle, who had not gotten to his feet. Possibly, she thought, he was too weak to do so.

"Uncle," she said, crouching down next to him and putting her hand on his shoulder, "you should go—" But she stopped short. Her head came up quickly, cocked to one side, as if she had heard something.

"What is it?" Erik asked in a low voice.

She turned her head slowly to look at her brother and said, "It's too late."

In one of the tunnels a gray form moved slowly, yet smoothly.

Outside the cave, Clint Adams and Ned Holt stopped. Clint looked back down the slope behind them, but because of the way it was slanted he could not see all the way to the bottom.

The ground was craggy up here, and they had lost the trail of the wolf, and of the people who had walked up ahead of them.

"Is this the cave, Ned?"

"I . . . I think so," Ned said, still looking around. "It looks like it."

"All right," Clint said, "there's only one way to find out. Come on, let's go in."

Vin Hacker had the same problem Clint Adams was having. From his vantage point he couldn't see who was up ahead of him. However, he did have the advantage of still being able to look down behind him, just in case someone else came into the clearing.

As if there weren't already enough people at this party.

Martika heard footfalls outside the cave at the same time her brother did, and while she knew it was not the wolf, she looked that way with concern.

Perhaps it was her father. Wouldn't that solve all their problems?

She was surprised when Clint Adams and Ned Holt walked in.

# THIRTY-EIGHT

"What are you doing here?" she asked.

"The same thing you are, I suspect," Clint said. "Is that your father?"

"This is our uncle," she replied. "What are you doing here?"

"I told you already," Clint said, "the same thing as you."

"All right," Martika said, standing up to face him, "what are we doing here?"

"Looking for a wolf." He looked at Erik and asked, "Aren't you?"

Erik and Martika exchanged a glance, but both of their faces remained impassive. The old man on the ground was staring down at the fire.

"Where's your father?" Clint asked.

"We don't know," Erik answered.

"Well, he was with your uncle, wasn't he?" Clint asked. "At least, that's what you said."

"That is right," Martika said, "he was with my uncle, but now, as you can see, he is not."

Clint studied the three Gypsies for a moment

then said, "All right, Martika, tell me about the wolf."

"W-what wolf?"

"You know what wolf," Clint said.

"How would we know anything about a wolf?" Erik asked.

"I don't know," Clint said, giving vent to his frustration. "To tell you the truth, I don't know how anybody can know anything about what's been going on. I'm only glad I came into it late or I'm sure I'd be stark raving mad by this time. Now all I want to do is find the answers before I *do* go mad. But I'll tell you what, I think if anybody has any answers, it's you people."

"Why?" Erik demanded. "Because we are Gypsies?"

Clint flicked his index finger at the man, too brief a gesture to be called pointing, and said, "That's it exactly."

"Always you and your people blame the Gypsies—" Erik began, but Clint wouldn't let him get started.

"No, no, no, Erik," he said, "I'm not going to let you turn the tables on me here. I'm the one asking the questions."

Erik made an impatient gesture with his hand and said, "Ask, but I do not guarantee that we will be able to answer."

"It was your mother and sister who convinced this poor man that he was some sort of wolf who walked like a man," Clint said. "Maybe you wanted the town to think that too. Maybe you were trying to protect the real culprit, the real wolf."

"Why would we do that?" Erik asked.

"I don't know," Clint said, with a shrug. "Maybe he's a pet of yours and he got out of control."

Clint was watching Erik's eyes when he said this and saw a flicker of something. Maybe he hadn't hit the nail directly on the head, but he'd gotten a piece of it. Something he said had touched Erik in some way. He looked at Martika then and saw her looking at her brother.

"How close did I get?" Clint asked. "The wolf is a pet?"

Erik looked at his sister and then, in disgust, said, "Tell him."

"The wolf is not a pet," Martika said. "He is our father."

For a full minute Clint stood there, unsure that he had heard right. After the minute was up and no one had said anything else, he decided to pursue the matter and see where it led.

"Who?"

"Our father."

"The wolf is your father?"

She nodded and said, "Yes. I do not expect you to believe me."

"Well, that's good," Clint said, "because I don't believe you."

"I do," Ned said.

"Shut up, Ned," Clint snapped. He had enough to handle with the Gypsies talking crazy. "Why don't you go outside and keep watch?" he suggested.

"For what?"

"For anything," Clint said. "Just keep watch and let me know if you see anything."

Ned shrugged and stepped outside.

"Is this the wolf's lair?" Clint asked the Gypsies.

"This is where he and Uncle separated," Martika said. "We are hoping that this is where he will come back to."

"And then what?" Clint asked. "You'll kill it?"

"We cannot kill our own father," Martika said.

"As you can see," her brother said, spreading his hands, "We have no guns with us."

In that respect Clint saw that the man was telling the truth. He was neither wearing nor holding a gun, and there was not one to be seen in the cave.

"You people intend to wait here for the wolf without a weapon?"

"That is right."

"And then what?" Clint asked. "How do you intend to keep the animal from killing you?"

"Martika will do that," Erik said.

"How?" Clint asked. Then he quickly added, "No, let me guess. She can communicate with the wolf, right?"

"That is right."

Clint nodded shortly. "Of course it is."

He was about to say something else when

Ned came rushing back into the cave.

"Clint?"

"What?"

"Somebody's comin'."

"Who?"

"I don't know," Ned said. "A big man, with an Indian girl."

Clint turned and frowned at Ned.

"A big man with an Indian girl?"

Ned nodded, and Clint hoped that the man wasn't seeing things.

"What's the man look like?"

"Big," Ned said, "with a beard, wearing a bunch of skins."

"Is he carrying a Sharps?"

"Yeah," Ned said, "a big one."

"Damn."

"Who is it?"

"His name is Vin Hacker," Clint said. "He's a wolfer, the best in the business."

"A wolfer?" Erik said.

"What is that?" his sister asked.

Clint looked at them and said, "A professional wolf hunter."

"And this man Hacker, he is the best?"

"I don't know of a wolf that ever got away from him once he started hunting it."

Now when the brother and sister exchanged a glance it was one of alarm.

"You cannot let this happen," Martika said. "You cannot let him kill the wolf."

"Your father."

"Yes," Martika said, "my father." She rushed

to Clint and said, "I can stop him. I can control him."

"The wolf," Clint said. "Are we talking about the wolf, or your father?"

"Both," she said desperately. "They are one and the same. You must believe me."

"Even if you don't believe us," Erik said, "you cannot let this man kill the wolf."

"Erik," Clint said, "I came here to kill the wolf too."

"We can talk about that later," Martika said. "First you must not let that man, the wolfer, kill the wolf."

"I don't know that I can stop him," Clint said, looking at Martika and Erik in turn. They were both nailing him with pleading looks, and he suddenly saw the very strong family resemblance. He hadn't noticed before, but Erik's eyes were as black as Martika's.

Martika's eyes, though, were by far the most arresting. He found himself staring into them and agreeing to do what she wanted him to do.

"Okay," he said, "okay, I'll talk to him." He looked at Ned. "Stay here."

"I'm comin'."

Clint didn't feel like arguing.

"Suit yourself."

# THIRTY-NINE

Clint stepped outside the cave with Ned behind him just as Vin Hacker appeared. He saw that the wolfer was carrying his Sharps, and that an Indian girl behind him was carrying a Winchester.

Clint stood with his rifle in his left hand, the stock against his thigh. His right hand was empty, hanging down by his gun.

Ned Holt seemed unsure of where to stand and finally decided to stand on Clint's right.

"Get on my left, Ned," Clint said urgently. He didn't want the man near his gun hand.

Ned scurried over to the left.

"If there's any shooting," Clint said, "you hit the ground. Understand?"

"I want to help."

"Good," Clint said, "you can help by hitting the ground."

"Clint—"

"Shh!"

When Hacker got within range, he stopped. Clint watched the Indian woman. She moved right up behind Hacker and stood just to his left. She did not hold the rifle like she was going to use it. Clint's guess was that if Hacker needed the rifle, she'd be ready to give it to him.

"Adams."

"Hello, Hacker."

"Saw you in town the other day."

"I saw you ride in."

Hacker nodded.

"Who's that?" he asked.

"Just a friend."

"Holt is the name," Ned said, speaking up nervously, "Ned Holt."

"Nice to meet you, Mr. Holt," Hacker said. He was thinking that it was nice to be able to find all of his targets at the base of this one mountain.

"You wolf huntin', Adams?"

"That's right."

"Didn't think that was your style," Hacker said. "Guess we're lookin' for the same wolf, huh?"

"Probably."

"Sure," Hacker said, "there's only one hereabouts I heard of."

"Is that so?"

"Yeah, that's so," Hacker said. "Way I hear it, this animal's got a price on its head—one thousand dollars."

While he was talking, Hacker passed his Sharps from his left hand to his right and set the stock of the rifle down on the ground. He was also turning his body ever so slightly toward the Indian girl. If Clint hadn't been looking for the move, he never would have seen it.

Clint's guess—and it was an educated one, based on experience—was that Hacker would not stop at killing them—and the people in the cave—if they stood between him and a thousand dollars.

"There's no wolf up here, Hacker," Clint said.

"No?"

"No."

"Not even in the cave?"

"If there was a wolf in that cave, do you think I'd be out here?" Clint asked. "No, we looked all through this cave. There's no wolf here."

"Well, my Indian girl here tells me different."

"The Indian girl?"

"Crow Woman, I call her," Hacker said. "She can walk all day, and cook, and she warms my blankets real good at night, but that's not why I keep her around. You want to know the reason I keep her around?"

"Sure," Clint said, "why not?"

"She can smell wolf." Hacker laughed. "Really, she can. From a mile off. She smells wolf now, and it ain't a mile off, it's right around here, so if you and your friend don't mind, I'll be going into that cave."

Clint knew that he should step aside and let Hacker into the cave. After all, there was no wolf there. For the time being, he was telling the truth. Yes, he knew he should just step aside, but he found that he couldn't. For some reason he stood his ground and went against his better judgment.

Martika had the *blackest* eyes. . . .

# FORTY

"Now, Vin," Clint said, "let's not do anything foolish here."

"You're the one being foolish, Adams," Hacker said. "You're standing between me and my wolf."

Hacker was continuing to turn slowly toward the Indian woman. He had a loose hold on his Sharps. He was going to release the Sharps and go for the rifle.

"Vin," Clint said, "let's talk about this."

Hacker wasn't listening.

"Hacker, if you go for the rifle the Indian girl is holding I'm going to have to kill you! We can prevent that by talking."

"Talkin's over," Hacker said.

He released the Sharps and shouted, "Now!" at the girl.

Clint cursed, drew, and fired before he realized that the girl was *not* giving the rifle to Hacker.

Hacker reached out for it, but his hands closed on nothing but air. By the time the wolfer real-

173

ized this, Clint's bullet struck him. Because he was turned to the side the bullet that might have struck his arm instead punched into his side and found his heart.

The girl moved out of the way before the big man could fall on her. He hit the ground and rolled just enough to carry him over the ledge. After that he simply rolled and rolled down the slope until he reached the bottom.

Clint turned and looked for Ned. As he had instructed, the man had hit the ground.

"You can get up now, Ned."

Clint holstered his gun and walked over to where the Indian girl was trying to look down the slope. Because of the angle, though, she could not see all the way to the bottom.

"I cannot see him." It sounded to Clint like a complaint.

"Why did you do that?" he asked.

She looked at him and said, "I wanted him dead, but I was afraid to try to kill him myself."

"If I had missed," Clint said, "he would have killed you."

She nodded.

"So you let me kill him for you?"

She nodded again.

He was about to say something else to her when they heard a scream come from inside the cave. It was bloodcurdling, and it echoed within the confines of the cave.

"Jesus!" Clint said.

He turned and started for the cave. Ned had already run inside. As Clint reached the mouth of the cave, he heard a sound from above him. At the same time the Indian girl called to him.

"Look out!"

He looked up and saw the brown form streaking at him from above. The wolf had launched itself and was in full flight, plummeting down at him. Clint reacted instinctively. He drew and fired, and then the wolf hit him. The animal weighed over a hundred pounds, and the force of the collision knocked him from his feet, and knocked his gun out of his hand.

As he hit the ground he rolled, lest the beast attack him before he got to his feet. He needn't have bothered. The weight that had struck him was deadweight, for his bullet had traveled straight and true.

Clint regained his feet and picked up his gun. He walked over to the wolf and prodded it with his foot. The animal was dead. He quickly went inside the cave.

"What happened?" he demanded of Ned.

Ned pointed to where the three Gypsies were standing. Just above them there was a tunnel. Erik was holding Martika, who was shaking.

He walked over to them and said, "What is it?"

"Up there," Martika said, pointing. "Up there."

Clint climbed up to the tunnel and went inside.

"A little further in," Erik called.

Clint walked until he came across the thing that had caused Martika to scream. It was a man, clearly dead awhile. He was a mass of blood and gore. It looked as if he had literally been torn apart.

It must have been Erik and Martika's father. So much for his having been a wolf.

# FORTY-ONE

Clint stayed one extra day at the Holt house, to make sure that everyone was all right. Certainly Ned Holt was all right. He no longer believed that he was a wolf who walked like a man. Now he believed that he'd been having a lot of bad dreams after talking to the Gypsies, and that during some of those dreams he must have walked in his sleep. Clint thought that was as good an explanation as any.

If he believed in hypnosis, Clint might have believed that Martika had somehow hypnotized Ned into thinking he was a wolf. Maybe she wanted other people to believe that he was responsible for the killings—mostly of stock, and one man—so that they wouldn't hunt for the wolf.

Also, he recalled his own inability to back down from Vin Hacker. All he would have had to do was let Hacker look inside the cave, but he remembered being totally unable to do that. Why? Because of Martika's black eyes? Had

177

she hypnotized him then? He chose to think not.

Clint still didn't know what the relationship had been between the Gypsies and the wolf. Could it be that Erik and Martika had really believed that their father was a wolf? As it turned out, their father had been killed by the very wolf they had been trying to protect.

The Gypsies had reacted strangely to the death of the man they said was their king. After Clint saw the body, Erik and his uncle went into the tunnel and wrapped the body in a blanket. Then they left, returning to their camp. They said they would now leave the area. Except for Martika continuing to look shaken, they betrayed very little in the way of grief or remorse.

Erik had said something to Clint before they left that he just didn't understand.

"Now he is free," Erik said of his father.

Clint decided that this must have been some sort of religious belief of theirs, that death freed a person.

Clint had the decency to bury Vin Hacker, although it wasn't easy. The ground was hard, and he wasn't able to dig very deep. Probably in the spring when everything thawed, some sort of animal would be able to dig him up and feast on his bones. Clint didn't think about that. He just did the best he could do for the man.

Crow Woman took everything Vin Hacker

had owned and went off on her own. Clint had
no reason to stop her.

Clint went with Ned Holt back to his house
where they told Libby and Rachel and Tad what
had happened.

"So you don't believe that you're a wolf anymore?" Rachel asked.

"Oh, Rachel," Ned said, with a sidelong glance
at Clint, "I never really believed that. . . ."

The morning he was leaving Clint said good-
bye to the Holts.

Libby took hold of both his hands and said,
"Thank you."

Outside he crouched down and said to Tad,
"It was an honor meeting you, Tad."

"Will you come back?"

"Maybe," Clint said. "I just don't know."

"If you do I'll be older," Tad said. "Maybe you
could show me how you shoot your gun then."

"Maybe."

Tad went off to do his chores as Rachel came
out.

"Do you have to leave now?"

"I have to go to town and get my rig, and
then I think I'll just keep going, Rachel," Clint
said. "I've already been here longer than I
intended."

"Well . . . I'm sorry we didn't get to spend
more time together."

"So am I."

She raised her chin and kissed him chastely

on the mouth. She had just moved away when Ned came walking out.

"Good-bye," she said, and went inside.

Ned walked over to Clint and shook his hand.

"Thanks for everything."

"No more dreams, Ned."

"I hope not," the man said.

Clint mounted up and looked down at Ned, who was looking puzzled.

"What's wrong?"

"There's just one thing that bothers me about all of this," Ned said.

"What's that?"

"Well," Ned said, "the wolf you shot?"

"Yes."

"It was brown."

"That's right."

"Well . . . the wolf in my dreams was gray, Clint," Ned said.

"Well," Clint said, "they were only dreams, weren't they, Ned?"

"Uh . . . sure, just dreams."

"Good-bye," Clint said, and nudged Duke into motion.

As he rode away from the Holt house, though, Clint remembered his first thought after he had killed the brown wolf. Staring down at the animal, he had thought that it wasn't nearly big enough to have made the tracks he had been following in the snow.

Watch for

**CHAMPION WITH A GUN**

151st novel in the exciting GUNSMITH series
from Jove!

*Coming in July!*

A special offer for people who enjoy reading the best Westerns published today.

# WESTERNS!

## NO OBLIGATION

### Mail the coupon below

To start your subscription and receive 2 FREE WESTERNS, fill out the coupon below and mail it today. We'll send your first shipment which includes 2 FREE BOOKS as soon as we receive it.

Mail To: **True Value Home Subscription Services, Inc. P.O. Box 5235**
**120 Brighton Road, Clifton, New Jersey 07015-5235**

YES! I want to start reviewing the very best Westerns being published today. Send me my first shipment of 6 Westerns for me to preview FREE for 10 days. If I decide to keep them. I'll pay for just 4 of the books at the low subscriber price of $2.75 each; a total $11.00 (a $21.00 value). Then each month I'll receive the 6 newest and best Westerns to preview Free for 10 days. If I'm not satisfied I may return them within 10 days and owe nothing. Otherwise I'll be billed at the special low subscriber rate of $2.75 each; a total of $16.50 (at least a $21.00 value) and save $4.50 off the publishers price. There are never any shipping, handling or other hidden charges. I understand I am under no obligation to purchase any number of books and I can cancel my subscription at any time, no questions asked. In any case the 2 FREE books are mine to keep.

Name _____

Street Address _____ Apt. No. _____

City _____ State _____ Zip Code _____

Telephone _____

Signature _____
(if under 18 parent or guardian must sign)

Terms and prices subject to change. Orders subject
to acceptance by True Value Home Subscription
Services, Inc.

**11393-X**